STAR WARS

MYTHS & FABLES

STAR WARS

MYTHS & FABLES

WRITTEN BY
GEORGE MANN

ILLUSTRATED BY
GRANT GRIFFIN

DISNEP
LUCASFILM
PRESS

LOS ANGELES · NEW YORK

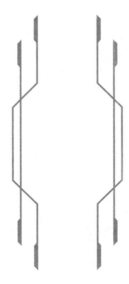

All rights reserved. Published by Disney • Lucasfilm Press, an imprint of Disney Book Group. No part of this book may be reproduced or transmitted in any form or by any means, electronic or mechanical, including photocopying, recording, or by any information storage and retrieval system, without written permission from the publisher. For information address Disney • Lucasfilm Press, 1200 Grand Central Avenue, Glendale, California 91201.

Printed in the United States of America

First Edition, August 2019

1 3 5 7 9 10 8 6 4 2

Library of Congress Control Number on file

FAC-038091-19179

ISBN 978-1-368-04345-8

Visit the official *Star Wars* website at: www.starwars.com.

For my young Padawans,
James and Emily.
May the Force be with you!
–G. M.

Thank you to my parents, Jean and
David Griffin, and a BIG thank-you to
my wife, Delaney Wray, for forever
keeping my spirits high.
–G. G.

CONTENTS

A LONG TIME AGO

IN A GALAXY FAR, FAR

AWAY....

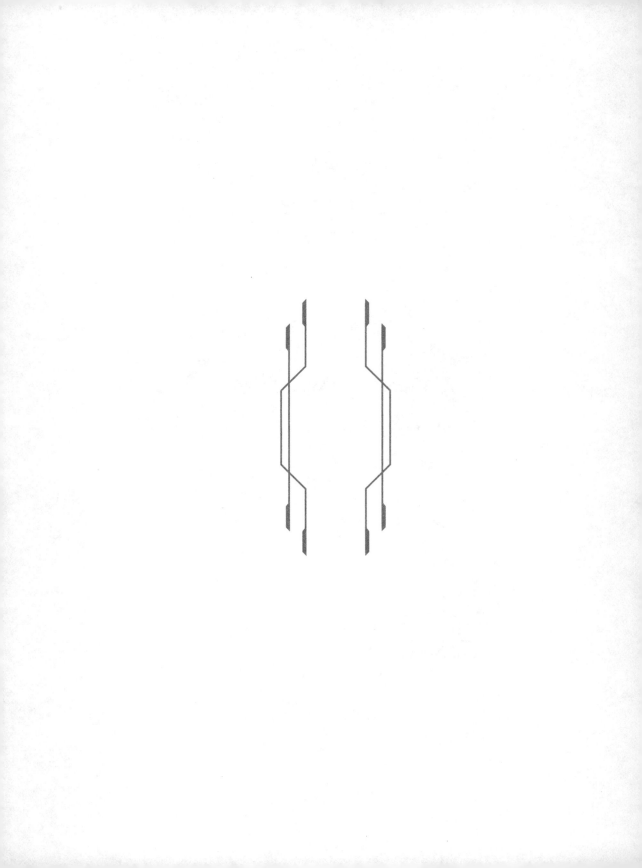

INTRODUCTION

ALL ACROSS THE GALAXY, there are tales waiting to be heard and stories longing to be told. Such legends are passed down through generations, spanning millennia, stretching to the farthest reaches of space as they are carried from planet to planet. For stories bind our universe together.

Whether whispered in quiet corners of cantinas, or shared while flying through the funnel of hyperspace, or simply told to little ones before they close their eyes at night, stories are for every soul who wanders this galaxy.

Indeed, true power resides not in armies and empires, or in blasters and ancient weapons of light, but in the tales we share with one another.

From the lowliest homesteads on forgotten planets to the glittering towers of bustling metropolises, from the hearts of smuggling dens to the tattered edges of

Wild Space, stories—regardless of origin or language— remain a powerful source of inspiration, instruction, enjoyment, and hope.

As time cycles ever on and the great wheel of the galaxy turns, such tales have proved, over and over, to be the seeds from which kingdoms and empires have grown, and the stuff from which great civilizations are built.

Indeed, stories are the rhythm of all languages, the root from which shared understanding might flower— told to the youngest, whispered amongst the eldest, and enjoyed by everyone in between, be they pilots or pirates, soldiers or spies, farmers or senators. Even creatures and droids pass on what they know to one another in the form of tales woven by time.

Some legends caution against unspeakable dangers and warn the unwary about straying too far down a dubious path. They demonstrate one's place in the order of things and make the vastness of the galaxy a little less uncertain.

Yet not all tales are cautionary in nature, and some in their telling instead point us toward possibilities and far-off lands, unimagined peoples and thrilling adventures. In this way, such grand stories encourage us to test our limits, to step into what our futures may hold.

For all across the teeming galaxy, every one of us is living our own story, treading our own, individual path. Sometimes we will stumble and sometimes we will stride, but no matter our destination, our tales will live on, told by those whose lives we touch, rippling out across the stars throughout the generations, because stories are immortal—eternal.

Here, then, are a few such tales, sought out from across time and space and carefully transcribed. Whether they are true or simply echoes of things that once came to pass, no one can be quite certain. Trust, instead, that before you lies more than a mere collection of words and pictures. And may you be emboldened by the power held within these pages. . . .

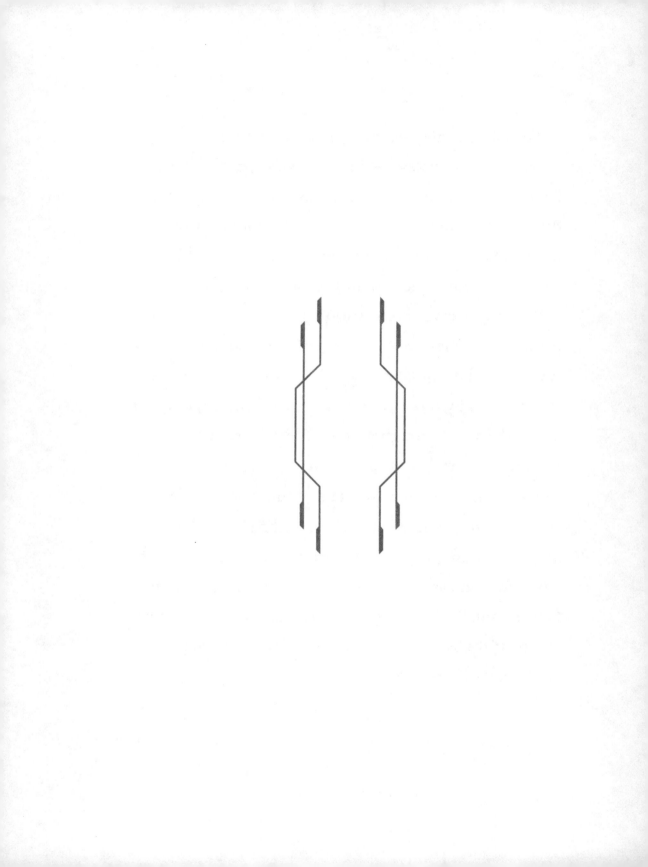

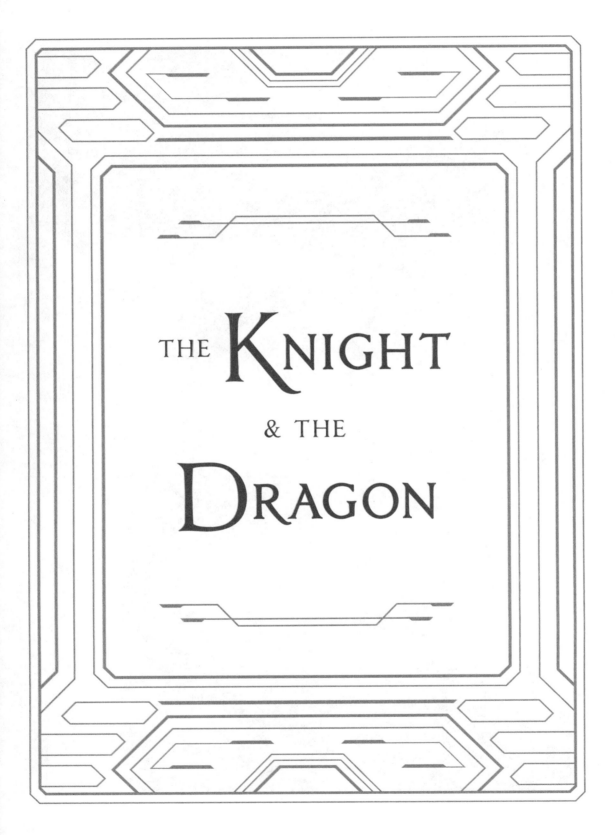

THE KNIGHT

& THE

DRAGON

THERE WAS ONCE A TRIBE of nomadic people on the distant, dusty planet of Tatooine who, for many months, had been terrorized by a fearsome dragon.

These were a simple people, with simple needs, who had for generations eked out an uncomplicated existence on the harsh desert sands, trading with the other tribes for water and sustenance, salvaging the wreckage left behind by those careless few who shared their world— those others whose lives unfolded in the noisy cities and spaceports, who tried ineffectively to hold back the sand rather than embrace its gifts.

The desert folk had little cause to visit those teeming cities, however, and although they had once roamed the rolling dunes in great caravans, they had found a place

to settle. They were at one with the land and knew that the desert itself would provide them with everything they might need.

So it was that these Sand People came to establish a village of their own, a place they might call home.

For many months the village flourished, and food and water proved bountiful as the desert offered up its gifts. The villagers, once so used to their endless migration across the sands, grew complacent and comfortable. Yet in their ignorance, they knew not that they had awoken the wrath of a great dragon, Krayt, that made its nest amongst the nearby dunes and called that domain its own.

Krayt was sly and knew that the people of the sand were in no way its equal in battle or cunning, so it devised a plan to rid itself of them. Just as the desert had provided for the villagers, it would provide, too, for the dragon. The people of the sand were numerous, and the dragon ever hungry; if it rationed them carefully, the villagers would sustain it for many months to

come. Soon enough, it would reclaim its domain from those interlopers—once they were all inside its belly—but dragons are long-lived and lazy, and Krayt saw no need to hurry.

Thus, it chose to begin with the villagers' plump livestock, which they held in large corrals on the outskirts of the village. Only then, when the entire herd had been consumed, would the dragon enjoy the taste of that which it so craved: people.

Thus began a campaign of nightly terror as the dragon—so large that the beat of its wings alone was enough to stir the sand into great storms that ravaged the villagers' tents—descended upon the village to snatch at the mewling beasts in their pens before hurrying away, back to its sandy lair, to feast. The villagers cowered at the mere sight of such a terrible beast, and in their fear, they made no move to try to prevent the dragon's attacks.

On the fifth day, however, the villagers were growing desperate, for they knew that if the dragon continued, soon there would be no livestock left in the pens to feed their children. That night, ten of the village's most trusted warriors took up their arms and went to stand guard over the pens, in the belief that, together, they might prove strong enough to scare the beast into fleeing, or even to slay it.

As it had each night before, the dragon came with the setting suns—a vast and horrifying silhouette, stark against the reddening sky. On huge wings it soared, sweeping low over the heads of the villagers, wheeling above them as they raised their weapons and took aim. Yet their weapons were ineffective and did not so much as scratch the beast. Far from dissuaded, it brushed the villagers aside with a flick of its wing and once more sailed away into the night with a squealing animal for its supper.

In such a way it continued for many days, until the villagers' livestock had all been consumed, and the Sand People themselves lived in fear of what the dragon Krayt might do when it returned to discover the pens empty.

Krayt, though, had planned for such an eventuality

and had secretly willed that day to come, because to a dragon, there is no sweeter meal than a helpless villager.

That night the dragon returned to the village to find the livestock pens had been abandoned. With a cackle of malicious glee, it turned to the village and beat its wings until the tents were swept away in a blizzard of sand and the people cowering beneath were revealed. For a moment the dragon seemed to linger, and then, licking its lips, it selected a young boy, whom it plucked from his mother's arms and carried away into the night.

The boy was not the last of his peers to be lost in such a fashion, for Krayt soon developed quite a taste for children. The villagers took to hiding their young in pits beneath the shifting sands, but the dragon was wise and had seen such tricks before. It dug up the children like wriggling worms, one to feast upon each night.

The villagers could stand for this no longer and elected a warrior from amongst their number, whom they armed with their most precious weapons, adorned with their strongest armor, and sent out into the desert

to stir the dragon from its nest. This warrior carried vengeance in her heart, for she knew the dragon must pay for the lives it had stolen, and she boldly claimed that she would soon return with the beast's head as a trophy of her victory. The villagers cheered as she strode off toward the horizon, and in their hearts, for the first time in months, they carried hope for the future.

That evening, the dragon did not return to the village. Cautious words of optimism were whispered around hearthstones as the villagers enjoyed their first night of peace for some time, and with the dawn, all agreed that the warrior must have been successful and the only reason she had not yet returned was that she bore the weight of the dragon's head on her return journey. Collectively, they sighed in relief and believed that the nightmare of their plight was over.

Yet evening rolled around again, and still the warrior had not returned. Optimism once again gave way to creeping fear, and sure enough, as the suns dipped out of sight, the dragon appeared on the horizon, and the

villagers realized that all they had achieved in dispatch-
ing the warrior was to save the dragon the trouble of
coming to the village for the previous evening's meal.
The campaign of terror began anew.

So it was that, in desperation, the villagers concocted
another plan.

Certain that the dragon would not be dissuaded and
would keep on returning until every last one of them
had been gobbled up, the villagers agreed that they
must find an alternative form of sustenance to offer the
dragon. The next day a small band of villagers set out
across the sands to where they knew a traveling band
of fellow desert folk had temporarily made their camp.
It did not please the villagers to lay siege to their own
kin, but the dragon had left them with little choice, so
the camp was hurriedly raided and the livestock stolen.
It was a small herd, but it would buy them time, so the
livestock were driven back to the village and penned in
the corral, ready for the dragon's return that night.

True to what had gone before, the dragon came with

the setting of the suns but showed little interest in the livestock, for it had enjoyed the taste of people, and livestock would never again satisfy its hunger. The villagers wailed as it plucked another of their number from the sand, for soon, like the livestock, there would be none of them left, and their plan to distract the dragon had failed.

There was only one recourse left to them: if the dragon wanted people, then people they would give it. Yet they would no longer allow the dragon to take from amongst their own, for they had already lost too many. Nor would they be driven from their newfound home, for the desert had accepted them and the months before the coming of the dragon had been the happiest they had known.

Thus, the raiding party that had set out the previous day did so again—only this time, they had a different quarry in mind.

It was two days before they returned, and they were pained by the knowledge of what those two days meant—that Krayt would have paid two more visits to the village in their absence. Two more of their people would have been lost. And yet, upon their return they were welcomed as heroes, for they had brought with them seven humans, captured on the outskirts of the nearest town and marched along the winding pathways through the dunes.

Most of the livestock corrals were empty, so the captives were herded into one such pen and bound, and upon the setting of the suns, one of them was chosen and tied to a stake outside the village boundary as an offering to Krayt.

At first the dragon seemed unsure of the new development—perhaps suspicious of the villagers' intent, lest they meant to poison it (in truth, a thought that had not occurred to the villagers, so desperate were they to save themselves). The dragon had, however, a most delicate sense of smell and was soon able to discern that the offering was fresh and juicy and wriggled just as well as all the others Krayt had plucked from amongst the villagers.

The villagers were overjoyed, for the dragon had been sated and their plan had worked. For the next three nights they continued in such a fashion, selecting one of the captives, pinning the sacrifice out on the village boundary, and going about their business while the dragon feasted. More raiding parties were raised, and further excursions to the nearest city yielded yet more captives. A solution had been found, and the people of the sand could once more go about their lives, assured that they had settled upon a means to appease the dragon.

Yet once again, the villagers had not counted on their actions invoking the wrath of another.

An old knight who had once been regarded as a mighty hero had made his home on the desert world, where he had long before been tasked with protecting a most particular treasure. The knight was retired from adventuring, and much like the desert people, he shunned the company of others, preferring a life of solitude and quiet contemplation while he went about his final duty. Nevertheless, the old knight was of an altruistic disposition, and upon hearing that people were being taken from the nearby town, he felt compelled to investigate.

The knight soon discovered the perpetrators behind the disappearances—for the desert folk were not subtle in their capture of the sacrifices—and, still stealthy from his years traversing the galaxy, followed the raiding party back to the outskirts of the desert village.

There the old knight learned the truth: that the villagers were acting in desperation to protect themselves from the dragon Krayt. Still, while he felt great sympathy for the villagers and all they had suffered, he could not allow such a thing to stand.

The old knight had not seen battle for many years and had long before discarded his armor in favor of simple robes—all the better to conceal his true identity from the many enemies who might yet seek him out on that backwater world. So it was that, upon descending from the dunes to enter the village, the old knight was derided by the villagers, who challenged him and bound him and tossed him into the pen along with the other townsfolk they had captured, for the villagers were blind to the truth and could not see that the old knight still harbored a great and terrible strength in his weary old bones. He would, they decided, serve as another sacrifice to the great dragon Krayt, despite his advanced age and tough, leathery flesh.

In his wisdom, the old knight played along with the villagers' games, until, penned in amongst the other captives and unobserved by the villagers, he shrugged off his bindings and set to work freeing the others from within. Soon the townsfolk had fled the pen, hurrying off into the dunes toward their homes, and the old knight stood alone, satisfied with his work and smiling.

As the afternoon light began to wane, the villagers returned to choose a sacrifice from amongst the captives but were infuriated to find only the old knight, kneeling silently inside the pen, his eyes closed in peaceful meditation as he awaited his fate.

With little choice, lest they sacrifice one of their own, the villagers dragged the old knight to the village

boundary and tied him to the stake before retreating to the safety of their tents to await the coming of the dragon.

Sure enough, as day finally gave way to dusk, the silhouette of the dragon, vast and ominous, appeared on the horizon, its wings unfurled to stir rolling clouds of dust as it sped toward the village boundary. It circled once above the camp, eyeing the old knight, laughing at the sight of such a poor victim.

Yet the old knight was wily and had once again slipped his bonds—for he had known the villagers would select him as their sacrifice—and as the dragon swooped low to pluck him from the sand, he stood and ignited his gleaming sword of light, which he raised above his head in warning, thus revealing his true nature to all who looked on.

The dragon, duly unnerved by the sudden alteration, wheeled in the sky above the village, roaring in frustration that what it had assumed to be another simple sacrifice had proved to be something altogether more complicated.

Krayt was an arrogant beast and knew that, despite the villagers' trickery—for surely it was they who had concealed the unlikely warrior beneath such humble robes—one man could be no match for a beast of its size and power. Krayt knew that it would not go hungry that night.

Thus began a dance of such elegance and ferocity that the villagers all emerged from their tents to observe as dragon and knight dipped and weaved—Krayt sweeping low with its whiplike tail and flashing talons, the knight ducking and leaping, the glowing blade of his sword humming through the air. He moved with a grace that belied his age, and the villagers knew at once, upon witnessing such a feat, that they had badly misjudged the man they had assumed to be a pitiful traveler from the nearby town.

For an hour or more the battle continued, and yet neither the dragon nor the knight had made a mark upon the other, so evenly matched were they in wit and skill. The old knight understood that, as well-fed and as strong as the dragon was, he could never defeat it in battle. Indeed, his display was designed to serve an altogether different purpose—for he soon began to tire, and he sensed the dragon's glee as he faltered in his feints and stumbled on the sand.

Krayt smelled victory and dove.

And the old knight lowered his sword of light.

The villagers gasped as the dragon swooped low, claws stirring the sand, jaws yawning wide to reveal a cavernous maw lined with ivory daggers. . . .

And then it *stopped*.

The old knight had raised his hand above his head, his palm held out toward the dragon, mere centimeters from where its tapered snout hovered.

The villagers held their breaths. The night had grown suddenly still. The old knight's blade flickered once, then blinked out. Then the dragon exhaled gently, issuing a contented sigh, before lowering itself slowly to the ground. Like a Loth-wolf pup before its mother, the dragon Krayt prostrated itself before the knight, its head coming to rest on the sand by his feet.

Tentative at first and then suddenly rapturous, the villagers began to cheer and hoot in celebration, for they saw that the old knight had cast a spell upon the dragon to quiet its mind, and in doing so, he had finally freed them from its reign of terror.

But the knight himself was not so easily placated, and he silenced the villagers with a look more fearsome than even that of the dragon. With a gesture, he bade the dragon to rise to its full height, towering over him, glowering down at the assembled villagers. He took a step forward and the dragon followed in kind, subject to his every whim, so mesmerized was it by his spell.

"The dragon Krayt is now under my thrall and, as such, will do only my bidding. No longer shall you suffer from its nightly visits."

The crowd began to cheer once more, but the old knight ushered them to silence again.

"Yet you have wronged the people of the town, for you have taken your pain and made it theirs. This, too, shall cease, for if you ever raid the settlements of others, I shall learn of it, and I shall return with this dragon and your village shall be destroyed."

At that the dragon stirred, spreading its wings as if to underline the old knight's point.

"Now go in peace, and return to your families, and enjoy the gifts of the desert."

Then the old knight turned his back on the people of the sand and slowly led the dragon away into the dusty night.

The villagers never saw the old knight again, or his dragon, but they remembered his warning well; thus, unique amongst the nomadic tribes of Tatooine, the villagers never again raided the settlements of others or took captives from the cities and towns of the desert world.

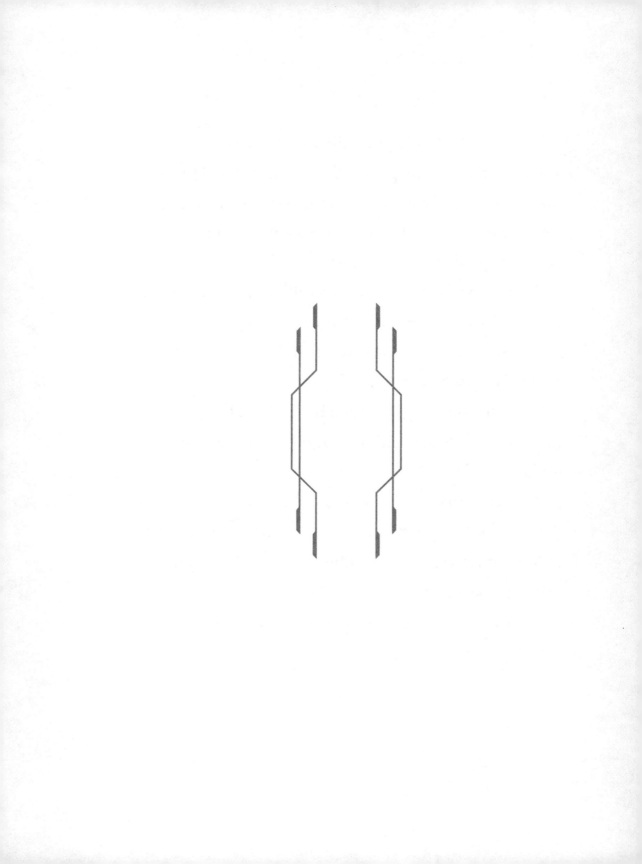

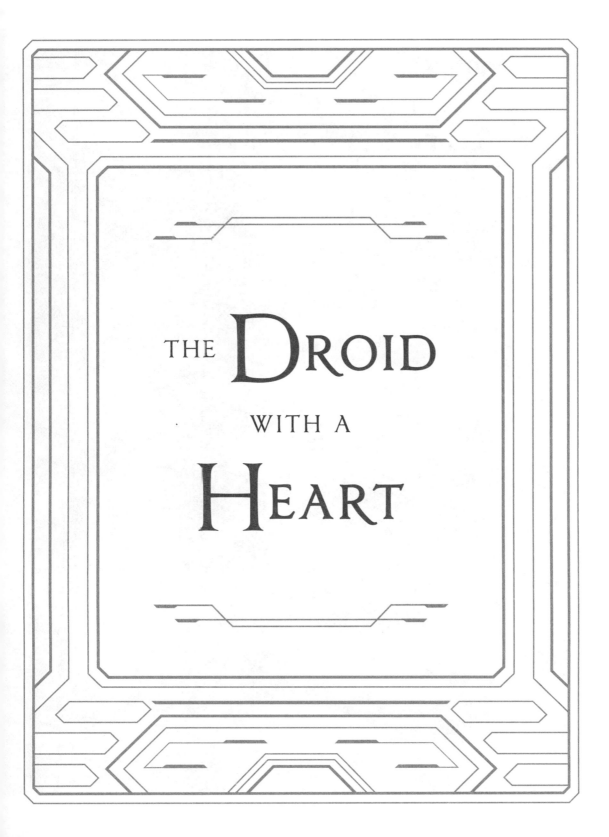

THE DROID

WITH A

HEART

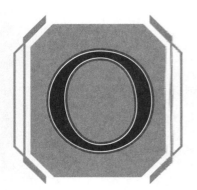

ONCE, DURING A LONG-ago war, there was an organic soldier who so admired the cool logic of the droids—and wanted so much to mirror their infallibility, strength, and power—that he took to replacing parts of his own organic body with a series of carefully crafted mechanical components.

At first they were simple enhancements—a cybernetic hand here, a data interface module there—but soon he came to see the full benefit of the new mechanical components and the way they enhanced his life. This was particularly true in battle, where the removal of nerve endings and easily damaged limbs meant he could take on even the most fearsome opponent without fear of pain or wounds. Nor did he have to hold back in his attack for fear of reprisal, as damaged droid parts could

be easily repaired or replaced, and the new components offered significant enhancements over his previous form. He had, for example, adopted four arms, rather than the original two he'd been granted at birth.

Victory in battle led to further modifications, and in time the soldier became utterly obsessed with the notion that he might eventually replace nearly all his "weak" genetic material and thus transform himself almost completely into a droid.

In such a way he believed he might enjoy the benefits of both the organic and the inorganic—all the strengths and versatility of a droid, with all the cunning, passion, and capacity for emotion of an organic life-form. The soldier would strive to become a droid in body while remaining an organic creature in heart and mind.

So the soldier continued in that fashion and, through the course of many years and many battles, adapted, tinkered with, and otherwise altered his own body until he was no longer recognizable as the person he had once been—more machine than organic, more droid than

man. The soldier was pleased, for he alone understood his true potential, and although he had the outward appearance of a machine, he retained some of what had once made him a living, breathing man. This, he believed, set him apart from all others—although neither organic nor droid found themselves comfortable in his company.

The soldier had achieved much in his life, and through the many campaigns he had fought on behalf of his masters, he had risen in the ranks, claiming victory upon victory. In part due to his sheer commitment to becoming the very best soldier he was able, he had made a mark for himself amongst the powerful men and women who led the Separatist movement.

Soon enough the soldier found himself promoted to the rank of general and given command of vast armies and fleets, for in him the leaders of the Separatist movement saw strength and power and the will to succeed. His gambit had paid off, and his success reinforced his belief that, in crafting for himself a new form, he had risen above all others. Even the Jedi shuddered at the mention of his name and feared joining him in battle, as none could match his sheer relentlessness and determination.

Yet, despite his martial success, the general remained unhappy, for though he had altered his body, he was not satisfied with his lot in life. In truth, he would never find peace or completion in the continued modification of his form, for deep down he sought escape, and no matter how much he might change *what* he was, he could never change *who* he was. Being a creature who was ruled by his heart, however, the general could never see that in himself.

Thus, this general who would be a droid was a tormented soul, and he expressed his torment by the only means he knew how—violence. The more the general altered his body, the angrier and more vindictive he became, lashing out at all those he perceived as weak, often destroying the droids placed under his care and leadership, for in some ways they reminded him of his own weaknesses. The general could not see the similarities between himself and those he bullied, believing he was not like the droids at all, that he was stronger, better, because of his organic heart.

So it came to be that, during the days of the great war between the Republic and the Separatists, the general was charged by his superiors with a most important task. He was to travel to the distant, frigid world of Alamass to deploy his vast army of droids in an assault that would destroy a strategic stronghold of the enemy. It was to be a dangerous and difficult operation, for the terrain was formed of frozen bergs of ammonia amidst vast unstable swathes of icy tundra. The general, however, had a distinct advantage over the enemy forces, as droids do not suffer from the cold like organic soldiers, and thus his armies were better equipped to face the difficult terrain.

The Separatist leaders knew that the general could be trusted to deliver on such a crucial mission, for his record was near unblemished and he was highly renowned for his tactical insight. All were assured of his victory.

Thus, the general led his fleet into orbit around the planet and dispatched probe droids to the surface to take the measure of the enemy.

There he discovered a large Republic army had been deployed in anticipation of the impending attack, along with scores of great war machines and armaments.

The Republic was not to be underestimated, for it, too, had great strategists and cunning generals, and despite the organic nature of its army, its members were resilient and had proved their mettle against the general's forces on many prior occasions.

Yet the general also spotted a weakness in the enemy's defense, for they had not anticipated an approach from the west, where the icy tundra gave way to turbulent floes and fast-moving tributaries, and where even the probe droids succumbed to the ice storms, treacherous ammonia vents, and alien beasts that lived in the murky, poisonous depths.

The general knew that to approach the enemy from that direction meant certain victory, for they had left

their flank entirely exposed. A swift strike would enable the general's forces to seize the stronghold and claim an early victory for the Separatists as further droids poured in from the south, pinning the Republic army in place. The general was certain it was the only way to break the enemy, to prize them out of their stronghold and destroy them.

There was, however, a downside to this daring plan: the victory would be gained through the sacrifice of many thousands of droids, as the droid army risked devastation marching across the floes, where they would be dragged into the icy depths or pummeled by the local fauna or corroded by the many ammonia vents that peppered the land in that area.

The calculated loss would be close to a third of the entire droid army, yet still the general pushed ahead with his plan, for he cared not about the impending losses. To him, the droids were simply machines, lacking the passion and drive of an organic heart and thus unworthy of compassion. He reasoned that, in deploying a mighty

force, he might stand to lose up to half of it during the march, but those few that survived would still prove enough of a surprise to distract the Republic army while his other forces moved in to deliver the finishing blow.

Once again, the general had set himself above those he had once aspired to be like, and in giving the order to deploy to the planet's surface, he condemned many thousands of their kind to ignoble destruction.

Now, these were simple droids, designed for combat and little else, and so had not the wherewithal or the capacity to challenge their general's orders. Indeed, these models were designed to never question the word of a superior officer and to obey all orders at any cost, without thought or reason.

There was, however, a most singular tactical droid amongst the general's aides, who plotted with and abetted the general in the day-to-day management of his troops. This tactical droid lived out its days aboard the bridge of the general's flagship and, if droids could feel envy, might be deemed to hold a most covetable position.

The tactical droid had, however, grown tired of the general's persistent bullying of the other droids on the bridge—for this droid had many times stood witness, in silence, as the general tore through his droid crew, igniting his blades of light to decapitate the unwary or breaking their servos over his knee. At times he had even wrenched heads free of their sockets before casting the unwanted appendages away with a ferocious roar. He carried on in such a fashion each and every day, taking out his frustrations on those around him until the entire bridge was littered with the remnants of the previous shift's crew. Droids quaked at the thought of operating in the general's orbit, and only the tactical droid itself had managed to survive for more than a few cycles in the general's presence.

The tactical droid had learned to always keep its head low, to avoid direct communication with the general whenever possible, and to swap its shift patterns with its fellow tactical droids to otherwise avoid as much of the general's company as possible. While the tactical droid felt a genuine nagging dismay at how the general treated its fellow crew members, it had always followed orders without question or delay, and avoided anything that might result in it being drawn into direct conflict with the general. Indeed, the general seemed altogether satisfied with the droid's performance, and in all its system reports its output was listed as exemplary.

That makes it all the more unusual that, on the eve of the deployment of the droid army to Alamass, that particular tactical droid made the active decision to commit a direct violation of its programming and orders.

To most droids, committing such a heinous act would be nothing short of anathema—a betrayal of the very worst kind—but this particular tactical droid had, during the course of the past seventeen cycles, been forced to witness the destruction of precisely one hundred and twelve battle droids at the hands of the general, and whatever limiters had been wired into its electronic brain were not enough to contain its seething anger at the sheer injustice of all it had seen.

Tactically, the droid knew that the plan devised by the general was sound; not only was it the most likely path to victory, but it was the *only* one. Yet that was not enough to quell the droid's rising anger at the thought of sacrificing so many of its kin, simply to award the general *another* victory. Orders were one thing, but this was a matter of principle. Surely the price of victory was too high? The tactical droid could not simply stand by and watch so many other droids marched into the jaws of destruction, let alone be the one that executed the order.

It considered this for a whole six seconds, running various simulations and models as it attempted to discern a new, alternative course of action and reason the various outcomes. None of them ended well, but there were those that minimized the damage.

Thus, when the final order was given, the tactical droid chose to intercede and, clear in the knowledge of what would happen to it when the general discovered its betrayal, altered the binary code of the orders being issued to the droid army, substituting an altogether different deployment zone, on a stable ice field over a day's march from the enemy stronghold.

Busily engaged in arrangements for the deployment of the second droid force to the south of the Republic stronghold, and not anticipating that his order might be challenged or disobeyed, the general paid no heed as the flotilla of troop carriers disembarked for the planet below.

Soon the droid army had been fully deployed and was slowly marching across the frozen tundra toward the enemy position. All reports from the surface confirmed that the battalion had been delivered as planned and was following its orders to the digit.

Satisfied in the knowledge that his plan was near guaranteed to work, the general gave the command to commit the second force to the attack that would pin the enemy between the two droid armies, and more ships made landfall on the surface, disgorging additional droids into the frozen wastes.

The second force fell in immediately, engaging the enemy, whom they expected to be reeling from the surprise attack from the west. The attack had not come, however, with the original droid army still half a day's march from the action.

As a result, the Republic army was ready for the droids and easily held position, falling back to protect the stronghold as the second droid army crumbled, breaking like a wave against the enemy.

Back on the bridge of his ship, the general, horrified to realize what had happened, was forced to call off his assault, pulling back what remained of the second force and ordering the original droid army to cease its march and retreat—for the Republic army had bedded in for a siege, and all hope of wresting control of the stronghold had been lost.

The tactical droid's deception had handed the Republic forces a resounding victory, and while there had been some droid losses during the battle, the impact on their numbers had been minimized.

The general was forced to admit his defeat—his first major failure—to his masters, and his shame was a greater wound than any that might be inflicted upon his mechanized body with a weapon.

The general learned, of course, that his orders had been processed incorrectly, although he knew not that it was an act of rebellion, deeming it mere incompetence, for he was blinded by his own prejudice and did not truly understand the nature of droids. Still he maintained a belief in his own superiority and could not ascribe motive to the droids he surrounded himself with, believing them to be nothing but machines, incapable of independent thought.

The general sought out the tactical droid, and, bellowing in righteous fury, in full view of its fellow crew members, he cut it into pieces with his flickering blades of light until there was nothing left of it but a series of glowing, smoldering hunks of metal.

Yet the tactical droid was duly revered for its act of defiance, and when the general stormed from the bridge

of his command ship, the other droids gathered its pieces, for they understood well what the tactical droid had done, saving many thousands of their fellows from destruction in the icy wastes.

The tactical droid was beyond repair, but its remains were fed into the recycler and became a part of many thousands of new droids, each of them carrying a small piece of it inside themselves. It was never forgotten, and tales of its bravery were whispered through the data-links and networks of the droids until, eventually, its story passed into droid legend, and all who heard it were proud to be droids.

From battle droids to droidekas, astromechs to protocol droids, all heard of the tactical droid's bravery, and it inspired many others to stand up against oppression. In due course the tactical droid came to be celebrated in the honor rolls of the Republic as a fallen soldier that had shown great compassion for its comrades—even though, unlike the general who had forever aspired to be like it, it had never really had a heart.

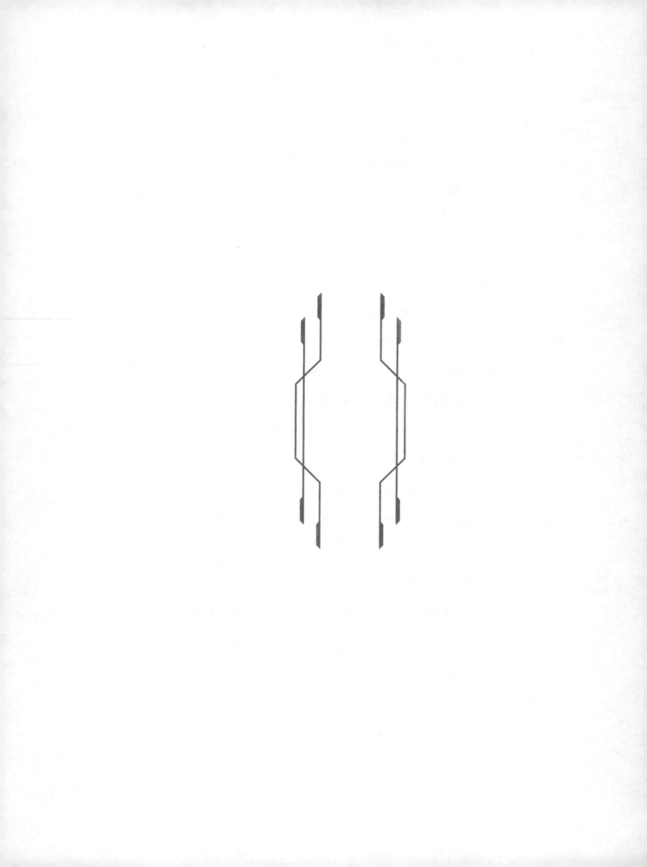

VENGEFUL
WAVES

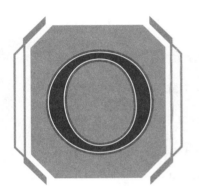

NCE, IN A TIME WHEN THE galaxy itself was still young and the stars burned bright with youthful vigor, there lived two races of amphibious people beneath the shifting waves of the planet Glee Anselm—the Nautolans and the Anselmi.

The Nautolans were easily identified by their pale skin in hues of green, gray, or blue, their glistening eyes, and the coiling tentacles that stemmed from the backs of their heads, while the Anselmi, although resembling their cousins, could easily be told apart due to their blue flesh and smooth pates, which were marked only by a pair of twitching antennae.

For millennia these two cultures had flourished, building great nations from the humblest of cave-dwelling origins, until they had raised glittering underwater

cities and colonized the ocean beds, from the deepest trenches to the coral-encrusted shallows that lapped at the uninhabited islands and landmasses above. Even the ocean spirit looked on in awe at their achievements and was proud of its children for all they had done.

For a thousand years there had been no disagreement between the two peoples—no war or infighting, no burgeoning fear or disrespect. Indeed, the Nautolans and the Anselmi were at peace and lived in harmony with one another and all the many creatures of the seas, from the greatest beast to the smallest crustacean. The empress of the Anselmi and the queen of the Nautolans had grown to be great friends, just as their mothers before them, and together they had fashioned a culture of mutual respect between the two species that seemed unassailable.

The two peoples shared much, cherishing each other's art, trading knowledge and goods and affection. Both understood the need to preserve the status quo, as balance in all things was essential to their continued survival, and so, too, to the success of all the creatures of the sea.

For this was the way of things on Glee Anselm, and the ocean spirit was duly pleased.

However, left unchecked, success breeds greed, and for the greedy, possession leads only to the desire to possess more. So it was with the Anselmi, for as their nation flourished and their needs became ever greater, they began to look upon the Nautolans with envy.

The seeds of this ill feeling took root and grew, for in the Nautolans the Anselmi saw others who had laid claim to what might be theirs—farm beds that were more fertile than their own and dominion over territory that curtailed the Anselmi's own expansion—and they began to dream of how things might change, and how the Anselmi might put their own future success over that of the Nautolans.

The Nautolans were a generous, giving people, inclined to share their wealth and bounty; so when ambassadors from the Anselmi empress came to petition the court of the Nautolan queen, she saw no reason to deny the Anselmi their wishes, and withdrew from the territory bordering their nation, gifting it to their needful neighbors. The Anselmi, instead of being grateful, saw only how swiftly the Nautolan queen had capitulated, and laughed at the Nautolans' naivety, thinking themselves clever and superior.

The Anselmi took the new territory they had received, and in it they flourished. Yet as their numbers swelled, so did their sense of self-worth, and all the while they wished for more—always more—and their hunger seemed never to be sated. For what the Anselmi searched for was missing in their hearts and minds, not to be found beneath the waves of the ocean or amongst the farms and cities of the Nautolans.

Time went on, and where once there had been nothing but peace between the two species, there was a growing sense of ill ease. As the Anselmi continued to expand and grow, they began to compete for resources with the Nautolans, and there were those amongst the Anselmi who believed they should simply take what was needed, irrespective of their neighbors.

While the Nautolans preached only peace, the philosophers of the Anselmi spoke of self-belief and the rights of the Anselmi above all others. The Anselmi people—for they had always been a proud folk and were easily coerced by the word of the empress—slowly came to believe a great untruth: that the Nautolans were weak and ignorant and less entitled, and that they had taken from the Anselmi the privilege and resources that should rightfully be theirs.

Where once there had been love and mutual admiration, there was festering hate, and the Nautolans knew not what they had done to inspire such resentment from their neighbors.

Soon the Anselmi had laid claim to more of the Nautolan territory, threatening violence, and while the Nautclans wished to avoid war, they did not easily relent, for they had taken the measure of the Anselmi and seen in them a rising arrogance that threatened the balance of all things beneath the sea.

Ambassadors were dispatched—for relations between

the Anselmi empress and the Nautolan queen had grown increasingly tense—bearing a warning from the Nautolan people to their neighbors. In it, the queen argued that if the Anselmi were to continue with their present ways, then the balance of all things would be upset and the living spirit of the ocean would be gravely displeased and exact punishment upon its children.

With an attitude of openness and admiration for her former friend, the queen begged the empress to cease her expansionist ways, for the empress risked the very downfall of the Anselmi, as no one might claim dominion over the oceans and its fierce and powerful spirit. The queen warned that the ocean spirit granted them leave to exist within its watery depths only so long as they strived to maintain the balance among all things, as well they had both been taught.

The Anselmi empress scoffed at such a warning, for she had grown so arrogant as to believe that the Anselmi's self-imposed superiority set them apart from the great beasts and the tiny fish, from their neighbors the Nautolans, and even from the ocean spirit itself.

Despite their arrogance the Anselmi understood that a war with the Nautolans would never be wise (for the Nautolans were great warriors, despite their disavowal of violence), so they sent the Nautolan ambassadors away with a message in reply: that the Anselmi people claimed dominion over not only the ocean but the lands above them, too. They would prove their superiority to the Nautolans, and afterward the Nautolans would be forced to admit the truth, and all of Glee Anselm would pay allegiance to the Anselmi people.

The Nautolans remained concerned for the welfare of their neighbors and pleaded with the Anselmi to reconsider, but their warnings fell on deaf ears. As one, the Anselmi dragged themselves from the ocean's grasp, heaving themselves onto dry land.

There, on a vast island in the middle of the ocean, the Anselmi found a place unspoiled by the touch of people, an island so large and so verdant that it might sustain them for countless centuries. The Anselmi had found

what they desired—a perch from which they might look down upon the ocean and its creatures and know that they had mastered all.

In the years that followed, the Anselmi adapted to their new way of life above the water, constructing a vast empire above the waves. Towering temples and spired cities were hewn from the very rocks, and their population grew to fill the shiny new streets and homes. They cared not for what they took from the land, for they had conquered it and it was theirs. They dug deep mines and stripped natural resources and fed upon the fruit and animals of the land until they were plump and lazy.

All the while, the Anselmi sneered at the Nautolans down in the cold embrace of the ocean and sent every ambassador back to them unheard. Soon all contact with their former neighbors ceased, and the Anselmi laughed gleefully at how high they had climbed.

Meanwhile, the Nautolans lamented the loss of the Anselmi, for they had once been loving neighbors and had lost their way. Still the Nautolans held to their own territory, living a quiet, peaceful, and happy existence, and the ocean provided for them. They wanted for nothing other than the safe return of the Anselmi, although they feared the arrogance of the Anselmi might yet prove their undoing.

Sure enough, despite the vast territory they had claimed, the Anselmi outgrew their island home, for they had built palaces and showgrounds for their leaders and stripped the earth of all its treasures. Just as they had once coveted the territory of their neighbors, they now looked in envy upon the ocean itself—for what right did the ocean have to cover the land?

Thus, in a great feat of engineering—the likes of which had never been seen before—the Anselmi raised a series of immense dams around their island, pushing back the ocean itself. They drained away the water to reclaim the land from the ocean's murky depths, and they built upon it, fashioning new, bigger homes and raising great statues in their own honor.

Once the work was complete, the Anselmi looked upon it with great pride, for there was the absolute proof that they were superior to all things on Glee Anselm.

Still the Nautolans sent ambassadors bearing warnings, but those ambassadors were turned away unheard, for the Anselmi had by then forgotten what it was to have neighbors, and all thought of balance had long before been dismissed.

Had the Anselmi heeded the warnings of the Nautolans, they might yet have come to understand the grave error of their ways, but in their arrogance, they were blinded, and in their blindness, they angered the ocean spirit.

Enraged, the ocean spirit rose up against them, hurling vast tidal waves and storms over the dams so they crumbled and fell, and soon the land the Anselmi had stolen had been taken back beneath the waves.

Yet the ocean spirit wished to teach the people of Glee Anselm a lesson, so the waves did not stop, crashing over the spires of the Anselmi cities, flooding the streets, toppling the statues, and flushing the people themselves from their homes.

It stormed without ceasing for days on end until, at last, the ocean spirit was satisfied and once again fell calm, its work complete.

Balance had been restored, and the Anselmi had been brought to their knees. Nothing of the island remained—a sunken domain, drowned beneath the tumultuous waves, all trace of the Anselmi empire gone.

The Anselmi, who had once deemed themselves superior to all others, had been reduced to a scarce few pockets of survivors, left to eke out an existence scavenging amongst the detritus of their former glory.

Deep beneath the ocean the Nautolans wept for the loss of their neighbors, for they had ever wished only to protect the Anselmi from themselves, knowing as they did that the balance had been disturbed and that the ocean spirit would not tolerate such a slight.

The Nautolans remained in their cities beneath the waves, always mindful of the natural balance, and never again did the people of Glee Anselm defy the power of the ocean or attempt to deny their place in the order of all things.

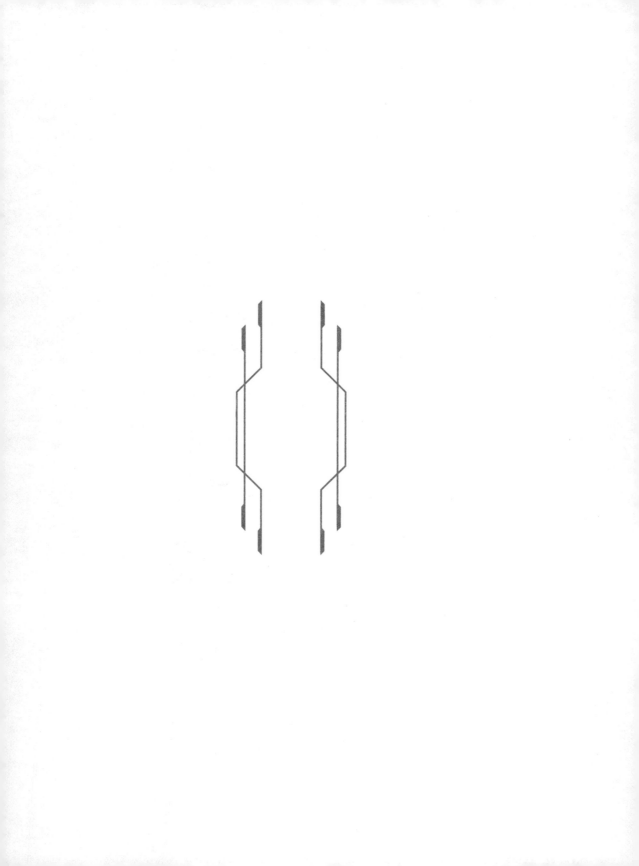

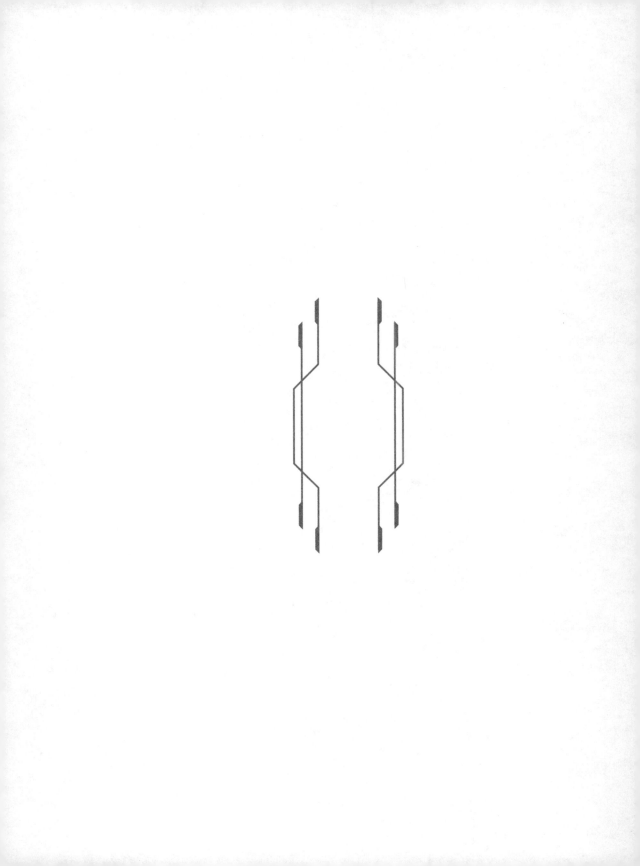

THE WANDERER

A LONG TIME AGO, ON THE planet Cerosha, before the city of Solace was destroyed by the vengeance of the Dark Wraith, stories were told amongst the people of a kindly wanderer who would emerge from the mist to aid the people in their hour of need, assisting them with their most difficult or dangerous plights.

The Wanderer always traveled alone, appearing in flowing brown robes, with a neatly trimmed beard and a mane of chestnut-colored hair that flowed over his shoulders. He carried a sword that seemed to glow with its own inner light, and he commanded the power of gods, for he understood the natural order of things and had power over all the creatures and the trees and the rising tide.

No one knew from whence the Wanderer came, or to where he returned when his work was done, and many amongst the people of Solace suspected he was naught but a specter, a conjured apparition, for he seemed only to appear when and where he was most needed, and none ever learned his name. While his visitations were few and far between, the mere fact of his existence offered the people hope, for they saw that there was goodness in the world and knew that they were not alone.

Three times the Wanderer was seen within the walls of Solace, and three times he helped the people overcome a threat that might otherwise have proved their undoing.

The first of these occasions was long ago, before the wars that tore the galaxy apart and long before Solace burned, back when it was the glittering jewel on the edge of the Boralic Sea, the pride of all Cerosha.

For many years the city had been a bustling port,

where traders from all across the known galaxy came to exchange their wares or to seek work or passage amongst the stars. The cantinas brimmed with patrons from the Outer Rim, and the people of Solace welcomed their visitors with open arms, embracing all with their hospitality.

The people grew rich, too, on the money they made from the traders, who brought wealth with them to Solace and spent credits in the city, seeking food and board and company.

Yet there cannot be light without darkness, and there were those in Solace who sought to encourage illegal trade and villainy and to bring the good name of the city into disrepute.

So it was that a group of nefarious pirates came to Solace, stationing themselves just outside the city in the craggy mountains, from where they could mount raids upon all the incoming and outgoing ships.

The pirates were a motley crew, comprising villainous sorts from many different worlds—Bith, Abednedo, Twi'lek, and human amongst them—and they took great pleasure in their work, demanding payment in cargo for safe passage in and out of the city and carrying out hostile raids upon the citizens, who cowered in terror at their coming.

For many months this regime continued, and the people grew desperate, for not only were the pirates slowly eroding all the wealth the citizens had accumulated over the years, but trade was becoming sparse as traders chose other ports to avoid paying the pirates' toll. Meanwhile, the pirates showed no sign of tiring, for they had amassed a great hoard in the mountains and grew lazy and fat off the proceeds.

In its desperation the city raised a small militia to tackle the pirates, but they were ill-trained and unprepared, and the pirates dismissed them easily, sending them scuttling back to their homes behind the city walls. It seemed as though the problem would never be solved and the pirates had made a permanent home on Cerosha.

It was then that the Wanderer made his first appearance in Solace, the day following the repelled attack

on the pirate base. No one saw him arrive, but all who encountered him that day spoke of the aura of power that surrounded him, and they knew that he was kindly of heart and mind.

The Wanderer spent the day walking the quiet streets of the city, speaking to those who had suffered at the hands of the pirates, hearing their tales of woe. If he had business there in Solace he kept it to himself, for he seemed to walk with no urgency and took time to speak with everyone who bid him good day. So drawn to him were the people that they emerged from their homes to witness his passing, and the winds blowing off the sea whispered of coming change.

That night, the Wanderer watched from a rooftop as the pirates carried out another raid, this time crashing a speeder into the city orphanage and stealing its donation fund, leaving the building a smoking ruin. Upon witnessing this travesty, the Wanderer promised to help the people and to relieve them of the pirate menace the very next day.

Thus, the next morning the Wanderer set out for the mountains, taking no provisions and carrying only the hilt of his glowing sword on his belt.

The people of Solace had gathered on the city walls to watch him go, for they knew in their hearts that one man could do nothing in the face of such villainy, and they feared for his life. Yet still they held out hope, for there was something about this wanderer they had never encountered before, a power that resonated in his every step.

For hours the people remained on the walls, until, as the sun began to set on the horizon, they knew they had been right and the strange wanderer who had come amongst them had tried valiantly to parlay with the pirates but failed, and they would never hear from him again.

Yet soon after, one of the watchers issued a cry, and in the distance, a lone figure was seen crossing the plain toward the city, leaving a cloud of dust in his wake. As the figure drew nearer, the people saw that it was the Wanderer, and they cheered.

The kindly man, with his strange mannerisms and even stranger appearance, returned to the city, assuring the people that they would never be troubled by the pirates again. Then, his business there complete, he turned and walked away into the setting sun, disappearing once more from their view.

True enough, the pirates did not return to the city the next day, or the day after, and soon a small expedition of volunteers set out from Solace for the mountains, whereupon they found the camp of the pirates had been abandoned and the citizens' own stolen goods left behind. The treasures were recovered and restored to their rightful owners, and trade once again began to flourish in the city as word spread and star-faring traders returned.

The Wanderer was not heard from again until many years later, when the people of Solace once again had dire need for his assistance.

The city had continued to thrive in the intervening time, and with it the population had grown

exponentially, and the needs of the people were far greater than they had ever been.

Thus, a large mining operation had been initiated, and huge drills had been deployed to open bore holes in the plains, from which minerals could be extracted for use in the city's forges and factories to help sustain the people.

Only, in drilling deep into the crust of the planet, the miners had woken a hive of creatures living in the hollows beneath the surface, and these horrifying beasts had spilled out of the ground to utterly infest the city.

These creatures were the size of small Loth-wolves, with hard, chitinous plating, long snouts, and vicious mandibles that crackled with a strange charge of energy that could disable a person with the merest touch. The creatures had burrowed into homes throughout the city, swarmed the sewers and alleyways, and worst of all, taken to feasting on children.

The people of Solace were afraid, for the creatures seemed unstoppable; they had found no weapon that

could penetrate the thick armor plating and no barrier that could halt the creatures' progress. In disturbing the underground nest, the people of Solace had lost their own homes, and nowhere was safe as the creatures swarmed from the depths like some terrible punishment sent to test their spirits.

All over the city people called out to the Wanderer for help, recalling stories of his previous visit and the miracle he had performed on their behalf. The Wanderer must have heeded their cries, for he came once again, unfolding from the mist like an apparition before the eyes of a child and his mother, somehow banishing with a simple wave of his hand a creature that had been menacing them.

Once again, the Wanderer took to the streets, forever inquisitive, hearing the tales of the unfortunates who had lost kin to the terrible jaws of the beasts, for the infestation had become unbearable and scores of children were being swallowed daily.

Upon seeing the extent of the city's plight, first

the Wanderer went to the site of the drills, where—employing his blade of light—he destroyed the mining machines, slicing effortlessly through their workings and severing their towering alloy shafts.

Then, returning to the city, the Wanderer chose a raised platform in the central square—the stage used by politicians to give speeches—and dropped to his knees, closing his eyes and folding his arms across his chest in silent meditation.

As the people watched—for word had spread, and the people had gathered—the creatures began to emerge from their burrows, poking out of the sides of homes and buildings and scuttling from the mouths of alleyways.

Soon a huge swarm of the creatures had gathered in the square, so many that they scrambled atop one another, chittering anxiously. All the while, the Wanderer kneeled upon the platform, his eyes closed as if in peaceful communion.

After a time the Wanderer rose to his feet and, with a final glance at those who had gathered to watch him

work, turned his back and walked off the platform, making a path through the crowd toward the city gates.

Sure enough, the creatures followed. Forming a grotesque, glistening carpet of swarming carapaces, they scuttled behind him in a long chain, the noise of their passing a thunderous roar.

The people watched in awe as the Wanderer led the creatures through the city gate and off into the chill of the night, back toward the derelict drill site. The creatures returned from whence they had come, and the people of Solace understood that they must never drill again, lest they stir the creatures once more from their nests.

The final appearance of the Wanderer came some years later still, when raging storms threatened to breach the city walls. Great tidal waves from the Boralic Sea crashed down upon the turrets and towers, washing briny water through the streets to carry away people, animals, and buildings in its path.

The Boralic Sea was a large body of water that served both the city of Solace and, to a lesser extent, the nearby city of Mock. Solace had grown up on the shores of the murky water and had for many thousands of years benefited from this proximity, as the sea provided a ready supply of fish and sea vegetables, and salt and rare spices were extracted from its depths.

Yet the storms that assaulted the city that year were like none that had come before, and many suspected unnatural forces were at play. Lightning crackled across a nightmarish sky, rain and hail thrummed upon rooftops, and thunder clapped so loud that it shattered windows and sent people cowering in fear. Yet this was as nothing compared with the vast waves that were thrown up from the sea, crashing again and again against the city walls like the engines of a siege, battering down the defenses in an effort to drown everything within.

There was nothing to be done, and as the walls began to crumble, the people knew that the city might be

doomed at any moment, should a big enough wave rise from the sea to wash the remaining mortar away.

Plans were made to evacuate, but the people knew their days were numbered, for to brave the storm without the shelter of the walls would mean certain death.

Yet the waves continued to rise, ever bigger, and they knew not what to do.

And then, as suddenly as if he had ridden in on the storm itself, the Wanderer was amongst them once again, and though he appeared the same as he ever had, those who saw him reported that he carried himself with a weariness that belied his calm exterior.

Despite his seemingly heavy burdens, he would not see the people of Solace come to harm, and ever defiant, he strode from the city toward the sea, his arms raised above his head. The crest of an immense wave rose to greet him and—to the amazement of all—the Wanderer held it back.

The wave rippled and roared in fury, towering high above the Wanderer's head, but all the while he remained standing on the beach, a serene expression on his face, his arms held high as if throwing up an unshakable barrier around himself and the city.

For nearly an hour he stood his ground, pushing back against the water, a battle of wills—but the sea was not to win that day, and as the storm finally broke, the waters calmed and retreated, and the wave finally collapsed, sloping back to the sea where it belonged.

The Wanderer broke his stance, and the city was saved.

Some say that he stayed to aid in the recovery after the storm, wandering the streets to drag the afflicted from their waterlogged homes, while others claim he melted into the dawn with the last patter of rain, that serene smile still writ upon his face.

Never again was the Wanderer seen by the people of Solace—not even when the Dark Wraith rose from the underworld to strike them down—and yet his story persists amongst those who survived the ruination, and his tale is still told beside hearths throughout the land, for the people of Cerosha know that he is out there still, wandering from world to world, helping those who cannot help themselves.

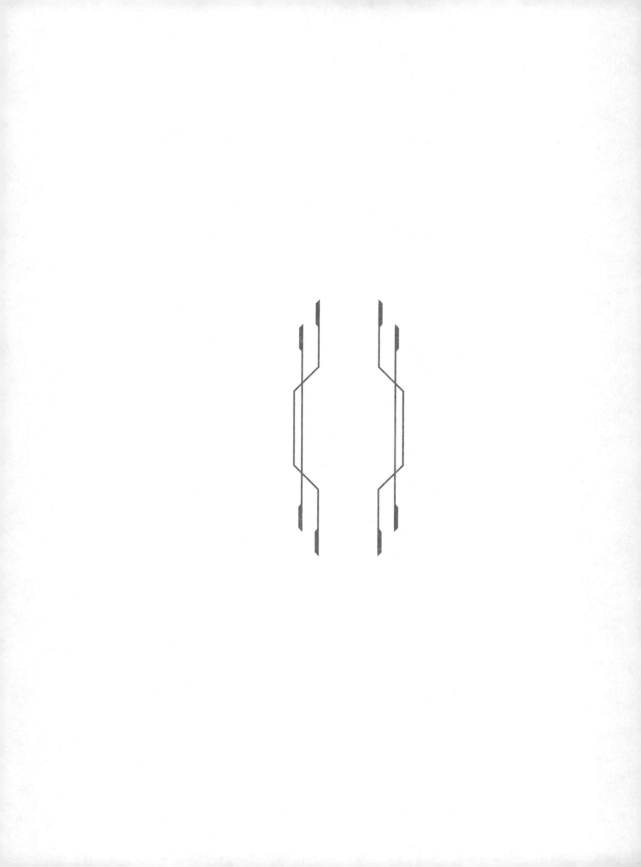

THE BLACK SPIRE

T THE VERY HEART OF Black Spire Outpost on the planet Batuu, there stands the bole of an ancient tree so tall and so black that all who pass in its shadow are compelled to look up in wonder and astonishment at its petrified boughs. It is whispered amongst the locals that, in its thousands of years of existence, the tree has witnessed so many terrible acts perpetrated by the settlers on its world that its very soul has shriveled and turned to soot—that it wished so much to retreat from the terrors it has seen that it left nothing but a shadow of itself in the world.

Yet wherever there is darkness there is light, and thus the tree, in its long life, has witnessed the advent of heroes, too.

One such tale concerns the adventure of a young girl

named Anya, whose story of heroism is near forgotten now, except by that towering spire, which clings to her memory as a shining beacon of hope amidst the darkness.

In days now long passed there lived a family on Batuu, out in the Saka homestead, away from all the bustle and noise of the village and its industry. Four siblings lived alone with their mother, for their father had died years before in a terrible supply-run accident, and the mother—ever true to the memory of her lost beloved— had continued to run the family grain farm in his honor.

The children and their mother were happy and lived a simple, peaceful life, taking their bounty from the land and visiting the village only rarely to trade food for goods. Yet being a single mother of four was a trying occupation, and oftentimes she would send her children out to play, wishing only for a moment's peace and quiet while she prepared the family meal or saw to the wash-ing of their clothes.

The oldest child—the only boy amongst three girls— had been born with a mischievous streak and, on such

an occasion of being told to take his sisters out to play, led them down to the edge of the Surabat River Valley, just as the sun was beginning its slow descent for the evening. The children's mother had long before forbidden them from venturing so far away from the homestead, claiming the valley was a dangerous place, but the children saw only the vast, unspoiled beauty of it, filled as it was with flowers and trees and brightly plumed birds. They laughed and cajoled one another, running through the long grasses, trailing their fingers across the stems of wildflowers, cavorting around the trunks of trees. They decided as they splashed through the river shallows and skipped stones across the shimmering water that they had found the perfect place for their adventures. They made a pact not to tell their mother of their visit and agreed that, upon their very first chance the next day, they would return to the valley to continue their game.

So it was that, after a restless night's sleep—during which the three girls planned their games in hushed

tones—the children finished their chores and bid their mother good-bye before heading out for the valley, giggling and nervous at their small act of rebellion.

As before, they found the valley deserted by all but the chirruping birds and a few colorful lizards that scattered as the children screeched and ran. The youngest child, Anya, found a shaded spot beneath a tree and covered her eyes, counting while the others ran to hide. Then she hurried, giddy, from place to place, searching them out. Soon enough she had found both her sisters—one had wormed her way into a hollow log, and the other had crouched behind a boulder in the mouth of a small cave. Yet, try as she might, she could find no trace of her brother. After nearly an hour of searching, Anya began to grow weary and called on her sisters to help her. Yet even after combining their efforts, they could not locate their mischievous brother, so good was his hiding place and so cunning was he.

More time passed, and the girls began to grow concerned. They called their brother's name, searched every

conceivable crevice, and climbed trees to get a better view of the valley, but *still* they could not find him. Had he fallen and hurt himself? Was he merely teasing them, refusing to reveal himself until they successfully sought him out?

As the light began to fade, the girls convinced themselves that, playful as he was, their brother had clearly left for home ahead of them and would no doubt be sitting with his feet up, ready to laugh at them for all the time they had spent searching for a hiding place he had never used. Yet Anya could not shake the nagging doubt that he would never be so cruel. Filled with uncertainty, the sisters set out for the homestead.

Upon their return, however, the girls found their mother alone, still stooped over the cooking pot, and there was no sign of their wayward brother. Terrified of what might have become of him, the girls hid in their room, where they remained until dinner, confused and afraid. Upon sitting down to eat, the girls' mother saw that her son had not returned for his meal, and she

inquired after his whereabouts—and at that the girls were forced to relate their troubling tale.

As she heard their story, their mother's eyes grew wide in fear, and, her voice choked, she told them the true reason why they had been dissuaded from ever visiting the valley. For there were whispered tales of children who had gone missing in that same valley, and rumors that the notorious criminal Sampa Grott had, on occasion, taken his sail barge there to lure the unwary aboard with promises of sweets and delicacies only to steal them away, back to his hidden lair, where they were put to work and never heard from again.

The mother was distraught, for she knew that her son was lost to her forever. There was no recourse; despite the desperate cries of the girls, there was little hope for the boy's return. They could never raise enough credits to buy the boy back from the slavers, for they were poor and lived off the land, and had nothing of much value to sell or trade. Nor were there any who would take up their cause, for Black Spire Outpost was a lawless place, and those in power had little time for local complaints or missing children. The boy was gone, and the family could do nothing but mourn for him.

Horrified, the three girls made a pact amongst themselves that they would see to the safe return of their brother, for while they heeded well their mother's warning, they could not just sit by and accept the boy's fate.

Thus, the following dawn, while their mother huddled in her bed still racked by sobs, the eldest daughter took up her late father's farming sickle and, urged on by her siblings, set out for Black Spire Outpost in search of her brother.

For the remaining two sisters, the day seemed to stretch interminably. They could think of nothing but the safe return of their siblings, and they paced the boundary of the homestead, watching the horizon for any hint of their coming. In the distance, however, they could see only the towering pillar of an ancient black tree, a sentinel from another age, staring back at them in tense silence.

As the light faded and the suns slipped beneath the distant horizon, still there was no sign of their absent siblings, and soon the girls were forced to admit the worst—that in going after their brother, their eldest sister had likely been caught by the slavers, too.

That night their mother wept still more, this time for the loss of her eldest daughter. She was certain the girl would never return and all her worst fears had been realized.

The two remaining girls tossed and turned, jumping at every noise, hopeful that every woot of a skindle or howl of a flintwing was the sound of their siblings finally returning to the homestead. Yet it was not to be, and with the coming of the dawn, the middle sister made her decision. She, too, would set out for Black Spire Outpost, to seek information about her missing siblings.

Anya, however, was less certain, for she worried at the thought of losing yet another sibling to the yoke of the slavers, and she begged her sister not to go. The other girl would not be dissuaded, though, insistent that she had no choice but to act. So it was that the middle girl took up her late father's blaster and, after telling Anya to remain at home to look after their mother, no matter what else occurred, set out in the footsteps of her elder sister to mount a rescue attempt of her own.

Anya could not bring herself to face her grieving mother, to admit that another of the woman's daughters had put herself at grave risk and set out to confront the slavers at the Outpost, so instead she passed the day in pilgrimage to the Trilon Wishing Tree, upon which she tied a knotted strip of fabric, hoping beyond hope that her wish might be granted and she might yet see the safe return of her siblings. She desired nothing so desperately as to be greeted by their beaming faces at the homestead that evening, to sit and listen in glee as they related their noble adventures.

Alas, when she arrived home, Anya found only her mother, disconsolate and withdrawn, a woman broken by the knowledge of what had become of her children.

At that, Anya fled to the woods, unable to endure the

sound of her mother's mournful cries. There, she curled up in the little shelter she and her sisters had built from woven branches and began to sob.

Soon enough, the sound of her weeping brought footfalls crunching across the forest floor. Anya had grown wary of strangers, and while she hoped in her heart that the newcomer might prove to be one of her siblings, she dared not peek out. Instead, she cowered inside the shelter, bringing her knees up beneath her chin, stifling her tears in the crook of her arm.

The footsteps stopped outside the shelter. Anya's heart beat so fast she thought she might faint. And then the figure appeared at the mouth of the shelter, stooped low, and peered in. Anya stared back at the newcomer in horror. It was a man, dressed in brown robes and wearing a dark beard speckled with strands of gray. Despite the kindly expression he wore, Anya was terrified of him.

"Go away," she told him, for she feared he was a slaver, grown bold by recent success and come for her in the woods.

"I come only to help," said the man. "I heard your tears and wished to inquire what was wrong."

Anya shook her head, wiped her eyes, and remained exactly where she was.

The newcomer was persistent, though, and went down on his hands and knees to edge his way into the shelter and kneel before her. "I mean you no harm," he said, and she could tell by his warm manner and the mournful look in his eyes that he spoke the truth. "Tell me your woes, for I might yet be able to help."

So Anya laid out her story for the kindly man, reciting the sorrowful tale of her brother and sisters, and what her mother feared had become of them.

When she had finished, the man seemed to consider her words. "You must go after them," he said, finally, with a long, plaintive sigh, "for you are the only one who can see your siblings restored to their mother."

Appalled by the very notion, Anya protested. If her older sisters had failed, how could she, a young girl, ever hope to stand a chance against the slavers?

"You face a turning point in the road of your young life," the man explained. "You must believe in your own strength."

The girl objected once more. "But I have no weapon." She explained how her eldest sister had taken her father's sickle, her middle sister had taken his blaster, and there was naught left for her.

"Ah," said the man, "but you are young, and small, and no one shall suspect you of great things."

Anya saw the truth in those words, and the prospect terrified her. Yet she was the only one left who could make a difference, for no one else would take up the quest in her place—not even the man, who smiled sadly at the thought but then shook his head, assuring her that the best path forward lay with her and her alone.

Still, she had no weapon, so the man took up a fallen branch and fashioned for her a small dagger from the dark wood. "This is just a toy," protested Anya as she turned it over in her hands, but the man was already retreating from the shelter and simply urged her on with a sad smile.

Anya hurried out of the shelter after him, but he had already gone, melting away into the darkening woods. Bemused, she tucked the wooden dagger into her belt and ran home to her bed.

The following morning Anya woke with fire in her heart, for while she remained fearful of the slavers, her fear had been overtaken by her determination. The man in the woods had been right—she alone could help her brother and sisters, for her mother had been consumed by her terror and grief, and the only remedy was their safe return.

So it was that Anya set out for Black Spire Outpost that morning, clutching her wooden dagger, intent on bringing the whole sorry episode to a close.

Anya had previously visited the Outpost with her mother but never before on her own, and the towering trunks of the petrified trees seemed dark and ominous as she approached, guardians that sought to usher her away, for she had no place wandering such a dangerous path alone.

It was there that she was drawn to a small, hollow fragment of a petrified tree that she found along the roadside. Something inside her sensed it would bring her good fortune, so she tucked it into her belt and continued on her journey, fighting back her fear, encouraged still by what the robed man had said to her the previous night.

The Outpost was bustling with beings the likes of which she had rarely seen—with long, craning necks or blue skin and head-tails or horns or shimmering metal bodies—but just as the stranger had said, no one spared her a second look, for they were all intent on their own business, and in her they saw only a child unworthy of their lofty attention.

For much of the day, Anya combed the streets of the Outpost, until at last, huddling in the mouth of an alleyway, tired and desperate, she overheard the whispered words of two ne'er-do-wells. They muttered in low tones about Sampa Grott and how one of them, a Gran, had been swindled by Sampa in a recent deal. The Gran made bold claims to his Ithorian friend, stating that he was heading directly to Sampa's Cradle to confront Sampa over his lost credits. When the conversation was finished and the Ithorian had slipped away, Anya set out to follow the Gran, tracing his path through the winding alleyways of the Outpost and beyond, deep into the foggy, uninhabited areas of the Surabat River Valley where no one ever ventured.

In the depths of the miasmic fog, Anya found herself in a terrifying place, filled with belching, oily smoke and mechanical grinding, where the hulks of huge machines were piled high like the skeletons of massive beasts left to rot in a macabre graveyard. Slaves worked in their multitudes, hacking and sawing and sifting and sorting, all beneath the watchful gaze of the slavers who had

taken them there. This, then, was Sampa's Cradle, his hidden lair, the dreadful place where he took all those he had lured onto his sail barge.

With great care, Anya sneaked amongst the towering shells of the broken vehicles, searching for her lost siblings. First she found her brother, forced to lift heavy crates of salvaged components and carry them across the yard; then she found her eldest sister, stooped over those same crates, forced to sift through them in search of dubious treasure; finally, she found her other sister, wriggling about in the crawlspaces of the wrecked ships, forced to fetch out armfuls of components that the bigger workers could not reach.

Presiding over all was a big, brutal-looking man with red skin, whom Anya soon discerned to be Sampa Grott himself. Upon seeing him, the girl knew immediately how her siblings had failed, for he was not a man who might be beaten easily in a fight.

Anya's heart sank. What good might she do against such a man with her slight wooden dagger?

Yet the girl was small and clever, and liked to hide. With the robed man's words still echoing in her mind, she devised a plan. Seeing that Sampa was filled with greed—for why else would he pluck slaves to work in his cradle when his riches were already so bountiful?— Anya concluded that he must have taken the biggest, most ostentatious home in the area, somewhere close by.

Sure enough, she found the place easily, and small and nimble as she was, she soon slipped inside through a crack in the shutters. The place was piled high with a lifetime's worth of salvaged treasures, or those bought on the proceeds of the work of slaves, and Anya looked on, appalled at his greed but dazzled by the splendor on display.

A lesser person might have abandoned the quest and made off with the treasure, but Anya knew well that such objects were, in truth, worthless and was determined only to seek the freedom of her siblings, for that was the far greater prize. Thus, she found a hiding place beneath Sampa's bed and waited.

Patience was her friend, and after a time Sampa returned to his home. He sat awhile amongst his treasures, counting his ill-gotten credits, but soon enough he retired to his bed, extinguishing the light and casting the entire room in shadowy darkness.

Anya, still patiently concealed beneath his bed, her heart thrumming, waited until she was certain the man had fallen into a deep sleep. Then, silently, she slid from beneath his bed and withdrew the little wooden dagger from her belt. Carefully, she crept closer to the bed, to where a shaft of moonlight from the window cast Sampa's face in a silvery puddle of light. With a trembling hand, she reached out and placed the tip of the dagger against his throat.

He opened his eyes immediately, panicked, but upon feeling the tip of the dagger against his throat, he lay perfectly still, barely drawing a breath as he attempted to fathom what was happening. He searched for her face in the darkness, desperate to set eyes on his assailant. Yet he could see nothing of Anya, and thus had no sense that she was but a little girl with a toy dagger.

"What do you want?" said the man, his voice pleading. "All of my treasures are yours for the taking if you might only spare my life."

Anya smiled, for she knew then that her plan had worked. "I am an assassin," she hissed, speaking through the hollow fragment of petrified tree she had found earlier, to disguise her voice, "and I have been tasked with ending your life. Yet your pleading gives me pause. There *is* something I would have from you."

"Anything," begged the man.

"Three children," said Anya. "The first, a boy you took from his hiding place in the Surabat River Valley as he played. The second, his sister, who came to find him bearing her father's sickle. The third, their younger sister, who came to find them both with her father's blaster. All have been put to work in your scrapper's yard. I would have you release them and send them

home to their mother. Do this, and then leave this world and never return. If you follow these instructions, I shall allow you to live. But know that if you fail in this task I shall return tomorrow and complete my work."

Sampa hurriedly gave his assent, and Anya turned and fled, slipping out through the window before the terrified man had a chance to rise and turn on the light.

Confident that she had done all she could, Anya struck out for home, traipsing through the night to reach her family homestead. Her mother was sleeping, so, weary and nervous, Anya went straight to her own bed and fell into a fitful slumber.

With the coming of the dawn, Anya rose to discover her mother in the kitchen, cooking up a large pot of stew, for her brother and sisters had all returned in the early hours, freed at last from the terrible clutches of Sampa and his slavers. No explanation was given for their sudden liberation, and none ever knew that their wily younger sister had been the cause of their salvation—none but the silent spires themselves, who watched over everything that occurred within the Outpost and beyond.

Sampa Grott was never heard from again, and rumor around the Outpost was that he had fled into the depths of Wild Space to ply his trade on new worlds, where his enemies might never find him.

So it was that a child with a wooden dagger came to be a hero, an ecstatic mother was reunited with her children, and everyone on Batuu was able to safely enjoy the beautiful Surabat River Valley once more.

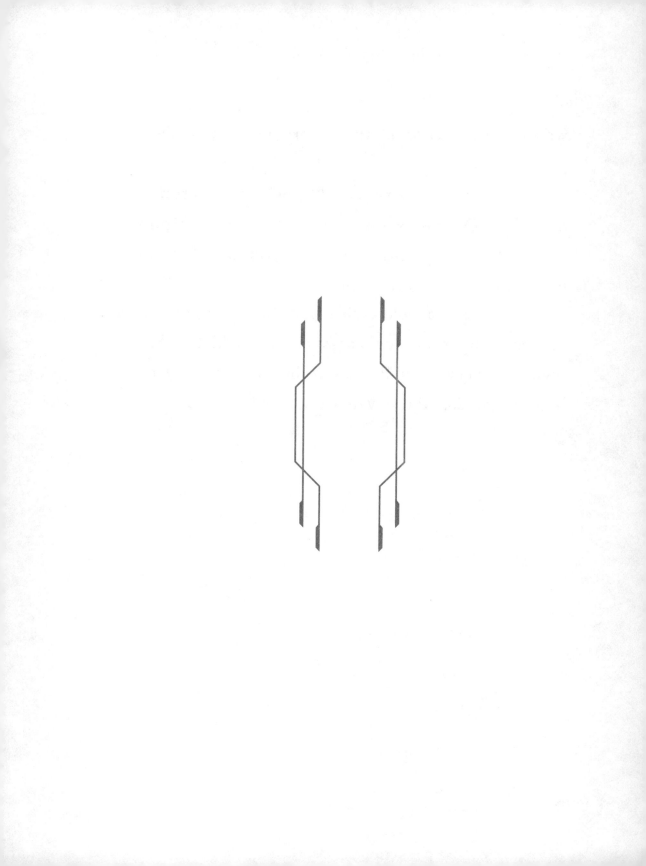

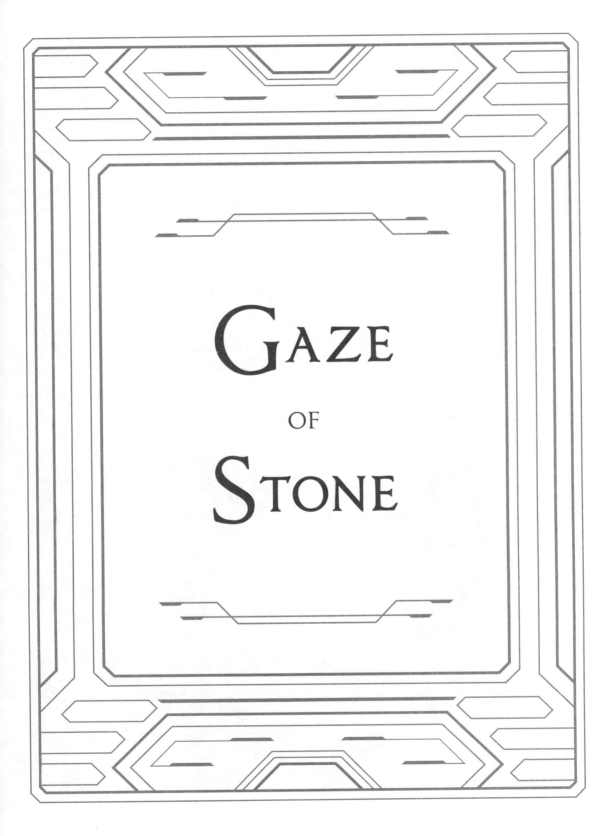

GAZE

OF

STONE

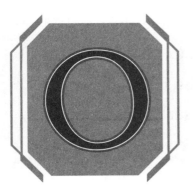

N THE DESOLATE PLANET
Moraband, high on a weatherworn
mountaintop, stands the statue of a
robed Twi'lek.

For a thousand years or more, since the ancient times when the world was known by the name Korriban, this lonesome figure has cast its gaze upon the bleak landscape below, and pilgrims venturing to Moraband in search of succor and forbidden knowledge have detoured to pay tribute to the unnamed figure, a man to whom they imagine great deeds to be ascribed—for he must have been a Sith warrior of startling renown to have such a monument raised in his honor.

Some such pilgrims have scoured the records and ancient texts for mention of the lonesome figure, but if his deeds were ever written, they have long been

expunged from the histories of the galaxy, for not a single trace of him might be found. All that is left for the pilgrims is the eerie, maudlin atmosphere they feel as they gaze upon the Twi'lek's graven face, and the stories they have since imagined, of how he once conquered whole worlds, imbuing himself with such power that all who knew him quaked in fear at his coming, for to see his face meant certain death.

There are others who claim that they have seen the statue weep an ebon tear upon the coming of the dawn, a single droplet rolling down its cold, hard cheek as if the stone were lamenting the passing of another day.

Thus, the statue has earned a variety of monikers, including the Weeping One, the Silent Watcher, and the Graven Lord, and many have theorized its true nature. None, however, has come close to the truth, for the statue's origins are far stranger, and more tragic, than even the most creative of pilgrims might guess.

The story begins with a boy, a Twi'lek named Ry Nymbis, who, since the very moment of his birth,

proved nothing but trouble to his mother. Even the midwives of Ryloth had sensed a strangeness in the babe as they'd bathed him and toweled him and handed him back to his mother, hurrying her home from the medical facility so they might not have to spend more time than necessary in the child's company.

Try as the mother might—for she wished only to love and protect her child as most mothers do—she had not been able to shake the ill feeling that the babe's presence inspired, even as he slept in his cot at night. The child's father, so affected by the aura that surrounded him, soon grew distant, playing little part in the boy's upbringing and welfare, preferring to take work away from the home, which caused a rift to form between him and his wife, eventually resulting in their separation.

As the child grew, aunts and uncles, cousins and playmates all stayed away, giving the family a wide berth, for they, too, sensed the strangeness within the boy. No one could quite put a finger on it—a feeling of deep disquiet, of *wrongness*, as if the child had been born ill-tempered, as if something foul had seeded itself in his very soul.

Outwardly, the boy showed no sign or physical manifestation of his bizarre character, but he understood all too well the effect he had on others and became solitary, maudlin, and quiet.

Eventually, after many months of hiding her shame, the mother grew desperate and wondered what might be done. She visited soothsayers and medics, shamans and doctors, and while all acknowledged the unusual nature of the boy and his bizarre influence on others, none could ascribe any particular condition.

Then, one day, close to her wit's end, the mother was approached by a robed figure who sought her out in the market. The man—an alien of a species she had never before encountered—seemed kindly and honest and, unlike all the others, who had been repelled by her child, said he wished only to help. He claimed he could explain the boy's affliction and knew what might be done to remedy the situation. She ushered the man back to her home, for he seemed to understand her plight, and there

he made predictions to her regarding the child's future.

The boy, he claimed, had been born with the capacity for great power—a connection to the living Force that underpins the universe—but, if left unchecked, could prove a danger to all who came to know him. Instead, what grew within him must be nurtured through the proper channels so the boy might learn to better control it, and only then would he, and those he had left behind, find peace.

The alien—whose name was Darth Caldoth— explained that he belonged to a great order and that, if the mother was willing, he might take the boy under his wing and allow the child to serve as his apprentice.

The mother was extremely conflicted, for she loved her child despite his affliction, but she saw the truth in Darth Caldoth's words. She knew that the boy would never be happy on Ryloth, where he would be shunned by those around him and never accepted for who or what he was. She feared that his powers might be put to misuse as his resentment grew and he learned to punish

those who had rejected him. She understood how he might become a danger to others, and thus to himself.

So it was that the mother agreed, tearfully, to allow Darth Caldoth to take the boy, for with his guidance she knew her child would flourish. She said her good-byes, and the boy was prized from her arms and spirited away in a shuttle, never to return home to Ryloth again.

So began the apprenticeship of Ry Nymbis.

However, Darth Caldoth's methods were extreme, and what he had seen in the child was a seed of hate that he knew could be shaped and molded. In that manner, the child might come to understand the ways of the Sith and turn his hatred into power. Thus, the child was first of all abandoned on the forest world of Simoth to a camp of slavers, who bred amongst their captives the fiercest, most bloodthirsty gladiators in all the known galaxy.

They took the child in as one of their own, tossing him into the pit to face a multitude of challenges, from slothkins to krastenanes, dianogas to—worst of all—other slaves. Yet the child somehow defeated them all, and as time passed he grew stronger and more agile, honing his battle skills whilst stoking the flames of his hatred. He learned to live for the kill, to trust no one but himself—to survive against all the odds. When he was wounded he embraced the pain and learned to grow stronger from it, and though the other slaves shunned him, they learned to respect him, and to fear him, for all that he was. The boy forgot about his mother and Darth Caldoth, and the pit became his entire world. He knew nothing but to fight, and in that bleak furnace he was forged—a coarse but powerful weapon.

For seven years the child worked the pit as a champion of the Simothian slavers, until one bright and clear day a ship came spiraling out of the sky, brushing through the canopy of towering malma trees to land on the outskirts of the slave camp. The figure that emerged from the vessel wore robes of black silk, and in his hand flashed a saber of burning red—the very color of Ry Nymbis's blossoming hatred. Within minutes the newcomer had effortlessly slaughtered the entire camp—slavers and prisoners alike—all save for Ry Nymbis himself, whom he forced to kneel in the mud before finally throwing back his hood to reveal his face.

Those alien eyes awoke memories in Ry Nymbis— memories of being taken from his home and abandoned on Simoth—and, enraged, he reached for his sword and rushed into battle with the newcomer, bellowing a challenge.

Yet, despite all Ry Nymbis's years of experience fighting the creatures and fellow slaves of the pit, Darth Caldoth was by far his better in combat, and he disarmed the young Twi'lek with a flick of his wrist, sending him sprawling to the ground, the end of one lekku severed and smoldering. There Ry Nymbis lay on the ground, subdued, the raging point of Darth Caldoth's saber hovering at his throat.

The Twi'lek's humiliation was complete, and Darth Caldoth explained that Ry Nymbis's real training could begin.

The trials undertaken by the young apprentice in

those early days were punishing and might have broken a lesser man, but Darth Caldoth had chosen his apprentice well, and his years spent in the gladiator pits had hardened Ry Nymbis, such that he thought nothing of taking another's life and faced the potential of his own death without the merest flinch. He had grown to believe in his own superiority and knew that, in all the galaxy, only his master had the power to humble him.

Together, the two traveled far and wide, undertaking missions with opaque purpose, searching the dusty stacks of ancient treasure hauls or the remnants of long-stilled battlefields in search of mysterious artifacts to add to Darth Caldoth's growing collection.

In an ancient, crumbling temple—a secret place, sacred to the Sith of ages past and carved from the black jade of a mountainside on a long-abandoned moon—Ry Nymbis was once again abandoned to his fears. For seven days and seven nights he stumbled through the nightmarish ruins, hounded by the specters of those who had plagued him when he was a child, by a twisted reflection

of the woman who had birthed him, by the living possibilities of the man he might have become, all fashioned into existence by the very power that flowed like burning magma through his veins. One by one he cut them down, freeing himself of their tethers to the past, nurturing the hate for them that swelled in his breast. He emerged from the trial half dead but exhilarated, and it was not long before he returned to his studies with renewed vigor.

Soon after, Darth Caldoth led his apprentice on the hunt for a saber of his own, stalking a lonesome knight through the electric mist of a night world until, confronting the warrior deep in the ashen swamps, Ry Nymbis choked the life from her and took her weapon, fracturing its heart until it bled freely in his hands.

Yet even as his power grew, so did Ry Nymbis's hate for his master, for Darth Caldoth had shown his apprentice that hate was the path to power, and Ry Nymbis knew that only Darth Caldoth himself stood in the way of his own rise to greatness. Secretly, he harbored

thoughts of destroying his master and taking his place, but he knew that his patience would be rewarded, for there was still much to be learned about the ways of the Sith.

Ry Nymbis's greatest trial was yet to come, however, for—confident that his apprentice was ready—Darth Caldoth led him on a pilgrimage to a distant asteroid in the cold depths of Wild Space where a powerful Force cult had built a fortress overlooking a fissure in the void. There, Darth Caldoth urged his apprentice to stare deep into the essence of the living Force itself.

The dark truth of his inner nature was revealed to Ry Nymbis, and after three nights of gibbering insanity, he rose once more, wiser and stronger and fully cognizant of the path before him.

Where once he had studied the art of combat and the power of hate, now he set out to study the mystic arts of millennia past, under the tutelage of his master. For Darth Caldoth had spent centuries scouring the galaxy for relics from the bygone ages, seeking out dark arts and alchemical practices forgotten by the living, studying those archaic powers so that he, too, might wield them.

Together, the two Sith pored over crumbling scrolls and stone engravings so old that their very existence had passed into myth, their languages forgotten, their creators long extinct. Wicked sorceries spilled from their fingertips, and even the greatest knights quaked in fear at their coming, master and apprentice both, for they had learned how to harness their hatred in ways not seen in the galaxy for a thousand years.

So powerful had they become that they were unopposed, masters of all they surveyed. And yet, as is the way with such men, Ry Nymbis remained unfulfilled, hungry for ever more power, for during his apprenticeship the Twi'lek had learned something other than hate: he had also learned envy and greed.

So it came to pass that Ry Nymbis became increasingly suspicious of his master, believing Darth Caldoth to be holding back in his training, reserving for himself

the most powerful of the teachings they had worked so hard together to uncover. Jealous rage burned within him, stoking the fires of hate, and Ry Nymbis knew that soon he would be forced to move against Darth Caldoth if he were ever to realize the full potential of his power.

Darth Caldoth was wise in the ways of the Sith, however, for he, too, had once been an apprentice and had long before seen to the demise of his own master, whose body lay deep in the crypts of the same abandoned temple in which Ry Nymbis had faced the demons of his past.

Thus, ever cautious, Darth Caldoth learned never to turn his back on Ry Nymbis, and the apprentice knew that, were he to tackle his master directly he would face certain death, for while he was his master's equal in combat, he had yet to access all the many rituals and scrolls that Darth Caldoth kept to himself, and thus the unknowable powers that might be extracted from them.

Yet his patience grew thin, for Darth Caldoth became ever more secretive, and where once he had encouraged the boy, he dissuaded the man. Ry Nymbis began to suspect the truth—that all that time, Darth Caldoth had used him, only taking on an apprentice so the master might benefit, that Ry Nymbis might assist him in securing the power he had so long yearned for.

So it was that a game of sorts began between the two Sith. Ry Nymbis was wily and worked to distract his master so he might steal into Darth Caldoth's chambers and search out the hidden scrolls, studying them hurriedly to glean what new information he could.

Darth Caldoth, wiser and older than the Twi'lek, allowed it, for he knew it would buy him time and that his apprentice had grown bitter and twisted and would not be discouraged from treading the path he had taken.

For many years that dance continued, and all the while Darth Caldoth delved ever deeper into the forgotten arts, and his status in the galaxy grew until even his name was not whispered for fear that in its speaking he might be summoned and appear to wreak devastation upon those who had dared call him out.

Darth Caldoth was not immune to pride, and such did his stature grow that he began to seek out those who might offer him fealty, to fashion an army of the dispossessed, an empire of slaves. And all the while Ry Nymbis watched and plotted, for he had grown tired of doing his master's bidding, and the time had come to strike and claim all that might be his.

The day came when, returning to Korriban, Darth Caldoth demanded from his apprentice a tribute—a monument, high on a mountaintop overlooking the desolate plains—that might serve as a warning to all those who dared underestimate his power.

So it was that Ry Nymbis devised a plan to erect a statue of his master, a permanent tribute to Darth Caldoth's enduring power. The statue would be so life-like, so true, that all who looked upon it might wonder if it were not, in fact, the real Sith Lord of legend. Indeed, Ry Nymbis would ensure the veracity of the statue by deploying one of the alchemical rituals he had stolen from Darth Caldoth's chambers—a ritual that would bind Darth Caldoth's flesh in stone, trapping him forever in a living nightmare. There on the mountaintop, Ry Nymbis would take the place of his master and his apprenticeship would finally end.

Darth Caldoth, however, remained wise to his apprentice's ambitions, and after hearing Ry Nymbis talk of the great monument he would unveil, he allowed himself to be lured to the mountaintop where his fate would be sealed.

Ry Nymbis was pleased, for his plan had worked and, as far as he knew, his master was unaware of the deadly plot—for Darth Caldoth, in his eyes, had given himself over to his own arrogance and in that arrogance had fostered ignorance.

As the two Sith stood upon the mountaintop, their robes stirring in the breeze, the Twi'lek enacted the ritual, muttering the unfamiliar words, feeling the arcane power rippling through him, his connection to the Force all-consuming.

Yet Ry Nymbis had not accounted for his master's

cunning, and the tribute was but another trial, a means by which to draw out the traitorous apprentice. Darth Caldoth had suspected his apprentice's betrayal and had prepared for it, altering the words of the ritual hidden in his chambers.

So it was that Ry Nymbis was destroyed by his own hubris. The ritual was a complete success, only, rather than turning the master to stone, it was the apprentice himself who succumbed to the creeping tide of calcification—from the tips of his toes to the ends of the lekku upon his head—until he had become his own monument.

Darth Caldoth had anticipated that chain of events, and his tribute was complete—a monument for all of time, a warning to those who might betray him, an apprentice turned to stone.

So it was that the statue of a lonesome Twi'lek came to stand upon a mountaintop on the planet Moraband. Even now, if any remain in the vicinity of the statue long enough, they might see a single black tear rolling down its cheek—perhaps the residue of the dark side ritual that once turned the Twi'lek to stone, or perhaps the anguish of the failed apprentice who has remained trapped on that mountaintop ever since.

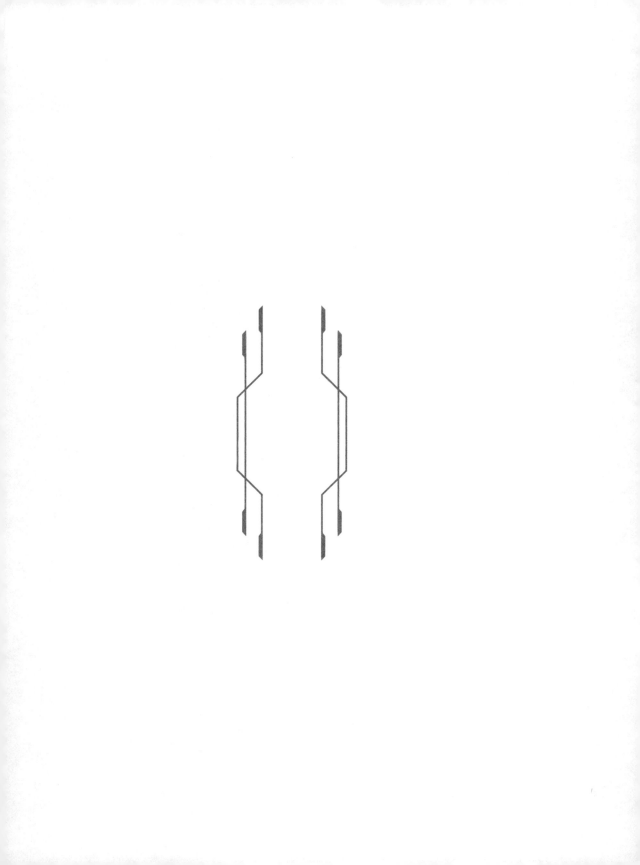

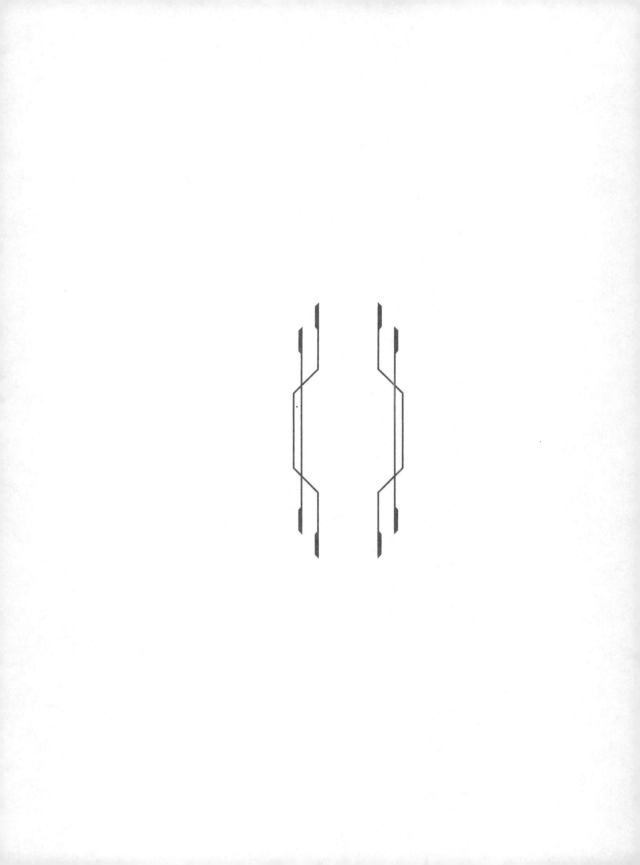

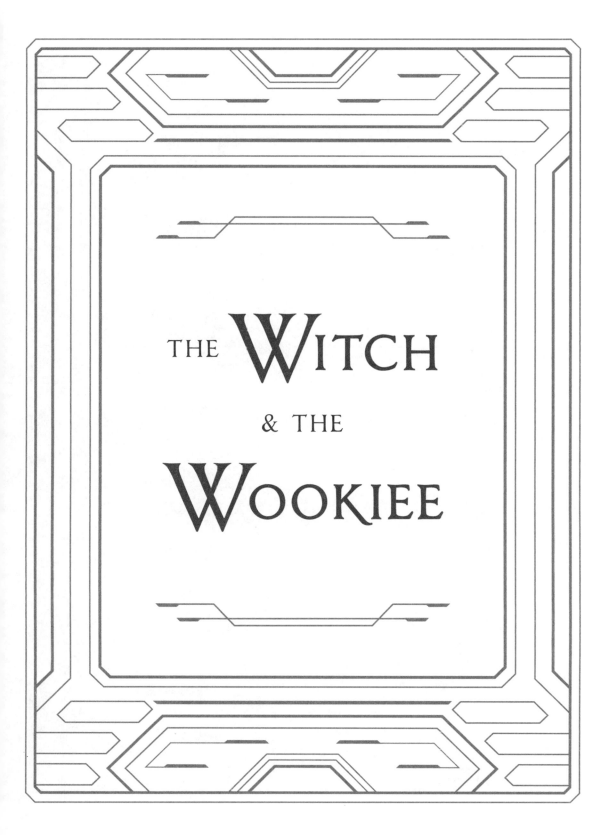

THE WITCH
& THE
WOOKIEE

IT WAS ONCE SAID THAT, SO powerful and all-encompassing was the will of the Emperor, the eyes of his agents could see into every crevice and darkened corner throughout the known galaxy and no deed could ever pass unobserved. Yet observing is not the same as *seeing*, and the Emperor's attention was forever drawn to matters of governance and the quelling of rebellion. Therefore, in many of those hidden places on the Outer Rim, seeds of indifference flourished, and those who had once lived under the Empire's yoke had become disillusioned by the iron rule of Imperial law and in their grievance seized the opportunity to carve their own path.

So it was that a small band of pirates came to find themselves aboard a stolen ship with a huge haul of treasure in its hold.

There is little honor among thieves, and these pirates—a bald, leathery-skinned Weequay named Marath, a tentacle-faced Quarren named Kalab, and a human named Houliet—had once been part of a much larger crew, but the lure of riches had proved too strong, and the three conspirators had betrayed their fellow criminals to make off with the treasure. As a consequence, they found themselves hunted not only by their former allies but also by the forces of the Imperial governor from whom they had originally stolen the treasure, and desperately in need of a safe haven and a suitable hiding place in which to store their ill-gotten gains.

Hounded at every turn by those who would have their revenge, the pirates fled from star system to star system until, finally, in the orbit of the planet Jhas in the system of Hoth, they found momentary respite.

Seeing that it was only a matter of time before their enemies caught up with them, the pirates devised a plan. They would hide their newly acquired wealth where none but them could find it—for they had each become enamored with the promise of the riches in their hold, and none could bear the thought of any other laying hands upon the treasure. They would then scatter to the distant corners of Wild Space to lay low for a time, until their trail grew cold and their crimes were all but forgotten. Then, when the moment was right, the three of them would meet again to recover the treasure, which they would split equally amongst them—assuming that they all still lived and had managed to evade those who sought them out.

So it was that Houliet—for she was the smartest and most devious of the three, and a former lieutenant in the military—settled on a small, uninhabited moon in the orbit of Jhas as the location for their hiding place.

The moon of Jhas Krill—it was whispered by those in the murky cantinas of the Outer Rim—was a foreboding place, where nothing lived but the swamp creatures and the twisted trees that grew amidst the foul bogs and steaming swamps. It was said that all who visited the moon disappeared, swallowed by the swamps

themselves, so the moon was given a wide berth by any and all travelers who went to the region.

Houliet reasoned—despite the trepidation of her companions—that such a place would prove the perfect spot to hide their treasure, for no one would think to search for it in such a grim and isolated location, and the rumors would do the work for them and dissuade others from seeking their fortunes there.

Thus, the three pirates made landfall on the small, unwelcoming moon.

Pirates, by their very nature, are not fearful people; so, upon disembarking from their ship—perched on a low, rocky plateau above the forest canopy—they were not dismayed by the strange, murky quality of the light or the shifting sounds of things moving deep in the bubbling swamp water.

As far as their eyes could see, the surface of the moon was wild and untamed, teeming with plant and animal life. There were no buildings, no suborbital platforms, no sign of anything at all, save for mile upon mile of

swamp and marshland, and towering trees, twisted and spiky, their branches swaying as they whispered to one another in the cool breeze.

They knew they had found the perfect place to stow their treasure—if only they could find a suitable cavern or hollow for it.

The ship and its precious cargo, they agreed, would be safe for a short while, and the automated defense systems would ensure that anyone who did follow them would be in for a nasty shock. Thus, the three pirates set out to explore the immediate area, each of them anxious to settle on a final hiding place before the darkness set in.

The three of them searched for hours, trudging through the mud, but still no caverns or hollows presented themselves. Thus, they were forced to delve ever deeper into the forbidding jungle, their boots stirring the swirling swamp water while unseen creatures slithered around the boles of trees, following through the undergrowth.

The jungle proved difficult to navigate, and the

pirates had a sense that even as they walked, the pathways through the trees were shifting and altering in their wake, branches twisting and knotting together to block their retreat. None of them gave voice to this fear, however, lest they incur the mockery of the others; so they continued, uneasily, ever deeper into the darkening jungle, each of them fearful of speaking out or attempting to return to the ship.

Night soon fell, and as the last of the light bled away beneath the treetops, the creatures in the swamps began to stir, dragging their lizard-like bellies from the dirty pools and streams, sliding amongst the fallen leaves that formed a slippery carpet on the forest floor. Shadows seemed to leer at them from amongst the trees, describing monstrous things in the darkness, leaving them jittery and nervous as they crept on through the jungle. They searched now for a place of shelter as much as a hiding place for their treasure, for the route back to the ship was long lost behind them, and they knew that to stumble onward through the dark was to invite danger,

for they might at any moment lose their footing in the boggy swamps or, worse, succumb to one of the terrible creatures they could hear snuffling through the undergrowth all around them.

Their way was lit by nothing but a single torch and the weak glow of distant Jhas, and as they forced their way on, shivering, even the beam of the torch began to waver.

"We must find shelter," said Marath, "or all has been for naught and we shall die out here, lost in the swamps, and in time others will find our treasure."

The others agreed, and, compelled by the thought that they might lose that which they had sacrificed so much to gain, they pressed on, even as the torch flickered and died and they were forced to navigate in near darkness, mindful of every step.

Now the jungle seemed like a small, dark place, closing in around them as they crept, and even the trees clawed at them with vicious branches, scratching at their arms as they stumbled blindly in the hope of salvation.

All around them, the slithering sounds of the creatures grew ever louder, ever closer.

It was then that Kalab spotted the soft glow of a light, up ahead amongst the trees. At first the pirates could not tell if it was the nearby flicker of a firebug or the distant light of a pyre, so disoriented were they by the oppressive surroundings.

Like moths to a beacon they were drawn to that light, stumbling from the path they had been following, through the press of branches and the frigid, ankle-deep water, until, at last, they came upon its source.

There, deep in the forest, was a small clearing, and in that clearing was a house.

The pirates looked to one another in sheer astonishment, for the moon was thought to be uninhabited, and not one of them could fathom who would even conceive of building a home out there, in the deepest, darkest part of the jungle, on a distant, unwelcoming moon.

Nevertheless, the pirates knew that they had been saved, for there they could take shelter for the night,

and, moreover, they had found just the thing they had been searching for—a place to hide their treasure.

First, however, there remained the question of who already inhabited the strange house, for a light was shining in the window and the scent of fresh cooking made their stomachs growl in hunger. The house was a modest abode, built from felled logs, with a single window and a single door. Smoke curled from a small stone chimney, suggestive of a welcome fire within. After their treacherous journey through the jungle, the pirates yearned for the warmth and safety it represented.

As one they peered through the lone window to see a woman sitting by the fire in a wooden chair, stirring a large pot of broth on the hearth. She was alone and looked content. After a moment the woman glanced up, sensing their presence at the window, and at once she hurried to the door to beckon them in.

She was a tall, thin woman with a pale face and short black hair, and she was dressed in billowing robes of red and black. She smiled warmly as she urged them into

the small house, closing the door behind them. There was not a hint of annoyance at their obvious intrusion on her solitude. Gratefully, the pirates hurried in from the cold to huddle near the warmth of the fire.

"I am Shelish," the woman told them, "and you are most welcome in my home."

The little house was cozy, and the fire cast deep shadows into the corners of the single room—but not deep enough to hide the glittering treasures that covered every wall and every surface. To their amazement, the pirates spotted strange totems cast in shining gold, silver goblets inlaid with precious gems, etched swords and ancient armor, priceless relics from the distant ages—treasures from across the galaxy. The woman had amassed such treasure that what awaited the pirates in the hold of their ship paled in comparison.

"Tell me, what brings you here?" prompted Shelish. "For I am not used to visitors and would understand what has brought you to my doorstep in this strange and lonely place I call home."

The pirates spun a tale of terrible woe, claiming they were hunted by fearsome pirates who sought to steal their ship and they had come to the moon to hide, only to find themselves lost in the darkening jungle, with nowhere left to turn and no way back to their vessel.

Shelish listened patiently and then, in turn, told of how she had long before been stranded on the moon after she, too, fled persecution and that, in all those long years, the three of them—Marath, Kalab, and Houliet— were the first visitors to come upon her home.

She promised them shelter and a bowl of warm broth, and she returned to her cauldron by the hearth, stirring and stirring the rich-scented contents. Not once did she ask for their help or intimate that they might rescue her by taking her with them aboard their ship.

The pirates were untrustworthy sorts, and despite the woman's kindness, they plotted amongst themselves in whispered words and secret code. Just as they had betrayed their former colleagues, so, too, would they

betray the woman. They resolved to make the most of her hospitality—to enjoy her broth and her shelter—before killing her and taking her treasure for their own, despite the fact that in the hold of their ship they already had more treasure than any of them could ever need. Such is the nature of greed, the affliction that strikes those who seek power and wealth above all else.

Shelish's house, they decided, would become their hiding place, and they would store their riches there, away from prying eyes and thieving fingers, and from that day they would never have to work as pirates again.

Seemingly ignorant of their plans, Shelish merrily set about serving up their broth, so happy was she to have company once again after all those years alone. The broth smelled wonderful as she handed it to them in little golden bowls, each one engraved with strange and abstract symbols, and which the pirates knew were worth more than the woman could ever conceive.

Hungrily they slurped down the broth, savoring its delicious flavor, so welcome after such a nightmarish

journey through the dark jungle—which, now they had reached safety, even the pirates had to admit had been terrifying. They sipped from goblets of rich, dark wine and feasted on succulent fruit, which Shelish told them had been scavenged from the nearby forest. All the while Shelish watched them eat, sipping only water as she sat by the fire in her wooden chair, smiling in pleasure at the pirates wolfing down her food.

While Kalab helped himself to seconds, Houliet asked Shelish whether she had any family—inquiring, in truth, to discover if the woman had any kin who might yet come in search of her, for the pirates wished to know that their treasure would be safe there, in that strange, melancholy house in the jungle.

Shelish shook her head. "I once had sisters, but now they are gone," she told them, "although I seek to honor them every day." Houliet smiled, for she knew that a woman alone in the world would never be missed, and neither, therefore, would her treasure.

When they had finished their meal and assured Shelish

that their appetites were sated, she collected their bowls and carried them to the other end of the room to rinse them clean.

While she had her back turned, Houliet gave Marath a signal, and in recognition he drew his dagger, rising to his feet with evil intent. On his face he wore a wicked grin, for he knew nothing but the ways of the pirates, and he thought only of the treasure that would be theirs once the terrible deed was done.

Yet Shelish was wise to the pirates' plot, having, in truth, suspected all along that they harbored murderous intentions, and as Marath crept silently toward her, she turned, a knowing smile on her crimson lips.

There was something in that smile that caused the Weequay to halt in his tracks, his knifepoint wavering, but even as he did so his attention was drawn to the shadows in the far corner, which had—as if agitated by the very darkest of magic—begun to stir to life.

In horror, the three pirates watched as the shadows swirled like living things, dancing and cavorting, until,

at last, they took form, swimming together to reveal the towering form of a shaggy-maned Wookiee.

Shelish laughed—a chill laugh that seemed to cut to the pirates' very souls—as the Wookiee took a step toward Marath, a low, threatening growl rumbling in its throat. Its fur was the color of shadows, and its eyes were bright and yellow and menacing. It was half again as tall as Marath, looming over him as it blocked his path to Shelish. It tossed its head back and roared, revealing rows of teeth like vicious daggers.

Shelish waved a hand, and swirling mists followed in its wake, encircling her in lazy rings, bright and luminous, a sorcerous barrier to defend her against attack.

The pirates knew that they stood no chance of overpowering the witch and her Wookiee familiar, and yet, as if compelled to see the plan through, or perhaps dazzled by the promise of treasure, Marath threw himself toward Shelish with murder in his eyes.

With an earsplitting roar the Wookiee intercepted him, knocking him to the ground with a swing of its

massive arm, sending the dagger skittering away across the floorboards and Marath sailing after it. He crumpled into a heap, moaning woefully. Shelish laughed again as the Wookiee plucked Marath from where he lay, holding the prone Weequay aloft like a trophy.

Houliet started from her seat, a blaster gripped in her fist, but she already knew it was over. The Wookiee was about to rend them limb from limb.

"Now, now, Owacchi," said the witch as the Weequay wailed in terror. "I believe our guests are just leaving."

"You mean to let us go?" said Houliet in stunned disbelief.

"You have eaten from my pot and drunk from my bottle, and that is everything you deserve. Now you shall leave this place and never return," said Shelish, "for next time I shall not be so benevolent."

The Wookiee growled in disappointment as he tossed Marath through the open door. The Weequay splashed into the swampy water beyond. The others hurried out behind him, neither of them looking back.

The pirates could not believe their luck. Soon they were far from the witch's house, and though none of them could quite shake their misgivings at how easily they'd gotten away, they were jubilant all the same. Dawn was breaking above the treetops, and the path to the plateau soon became clear. The creatures that had slithered unseen in the darkness had sloped back to their watery lairs, and the pirates' journey to the ship remained uncontested. By the time they climbed into the vessel, they were even laughing about the look on Marath's face as the Wookiee had pitched him out the door. Soon, they joked, they would be telling that story in cantinas all across Wild Space.

"What I wouldn't give for that witch's treasure," said Kalab, still thinking of the golden bowls and ancient totems. But they all knew the unspoken truth—that if it weren't for the witch's intervention, the Wookiee would have torn them limb from limb, and there would have been nothing they could do to stop it. Any thought of returning to the house had fled their minds, so grateful

were they to be safely in their ship. Soon they would be away from the dreadful moon and the horrors it harbored in its jungle, and they would find another world, somewhere more hospitable, where they could hide their ill-gotten treasure.

"Still," said Houliet, strolling into the hold to take in the heaped treasure with a sweep of her arms, "at least we have all of this." With a laugh, she grabbed for a golden goblet, holding it up to the others as if to make a toast. "With this . . ." Her voice trailed off, her face frozen in horrified shock as the three pirates all watched the goblet slowly crumble and turn to dust in her grasp.

"What?" Frantic, wide-eyed, Houliet reached for another, murmuring in abject horror as that, too, disintegrated in her hands, becoming naught but streams of dust that trickled through her fingers.

The others rushed forward, grabbing handfuls of the treasure, but the effect was the same, and everything from coins to jewels to relics turned to dust.

"The witch," said Marath. "She cursed us."

"'Everything you deserve,'" said Houliet, tears streaming down her cheeks as more of the treasure disintegrated in her outstretched hands.

Wreathed in shadows, Shelish watched from the window of her house as the pirates' ship ascended above the treetops, then blasted away into space. A wicked smile drew her lips tight across her face, for all around her, shimmering into being as if materializing from the dust itself, was the treasure from the pirates' hold, the glittering hoard filling her tiny house. She turned to her Wookiee companion and laughed.

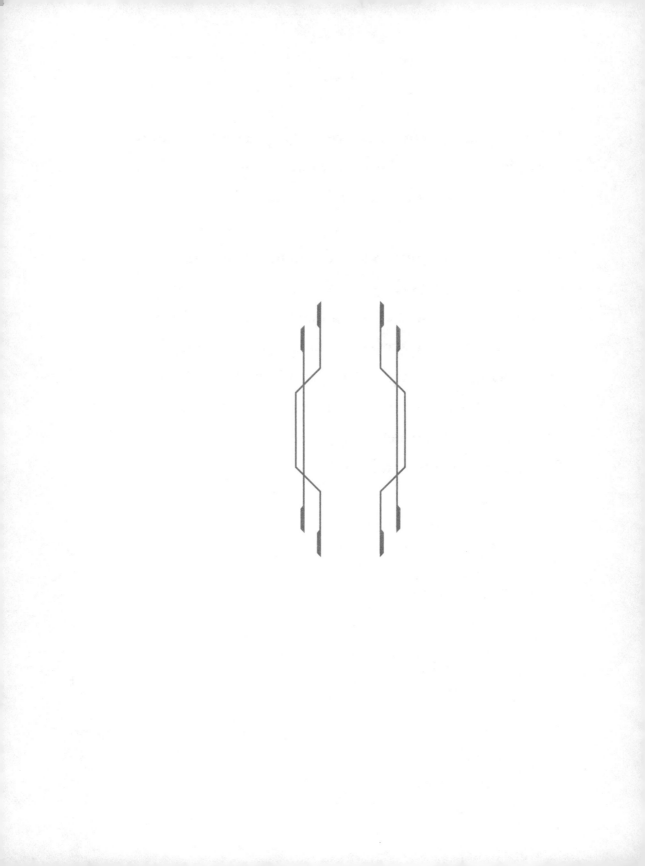

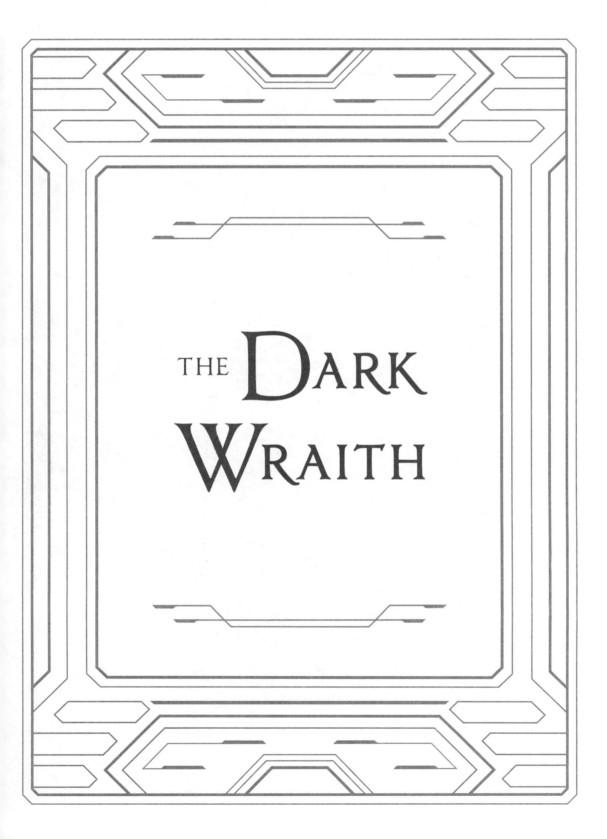

THE DARK WRAITH

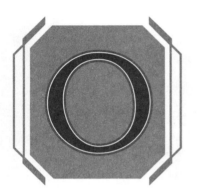

N THE PLANET CEROSHA, close to the Boralic Sea, stand the vast, desolate ruins of a once-great city, uninhabited and haunted by the tortured spirits of those who once lived amongst its toppled spires.

Those who live in the nearby city of Mock can still, on a clear day, glimpse the ruins from their windows, and all who travel the dusty roads that once served the city now give the area a wide berth, for it is a forlorn place, a melancholy graveyard, and it is said that those who do venture into its abandoned streets never emerge the same as they once were.

In all the time that has passed since the city's destruction, none of the governors, senators, or generals who

have ruled over the planet have ever looked to redevelop the land, nor have they considered rebuilding what was once there, for the ruins of the city of Solace stand as a stark reminder of what happens to those who misbehave.

Indeed, it is whispered that all one can hear as one passes by the tumbledown gates is the harsh, ragged breath of the Dark Wraith, who once destroyed the city and who may still lurk amongst the broken towers and fallen buildings, waiting to preside in judgment over any who dare trespass in his shadowy domain.

Stories have long abounded on Cerosha of this mysterious Dark Wraith, who for years has stalked the chill nights, seeking out all those who have dared to step out of line, be they children or adults. The Dark Wraith recognizes no difference and comes to issue punishment all the same. Some say he lurks in the corner of every child's eye, just out of view. Others claim that he resides in the pooled shadows at the foot of every bed, in the mouths of silent alleyways or behind every closed door, in the murky reflection at the edge of a stained mirror, or just over one's shoulder, watching every move. If he is to catch you, to witness your misbehavior himself, he will punish you swiftly with a flash of his deadly volcanic arm. No one who misbehaves is safe—be they in Mock or Cairos or any other city upon the fertile surface of Cerosha.

The woeful tale of Solace's fall can be charted—those in nearby Mock have been heard to say—through the tales of the individuals who misbehaved so badly that the Dark Wraith grew furious, his warnings ignored, and in his anger lashed out and destroyed the city entire.

One such tale concerns a boy named Jherl, who—no matter what his parents said or did—refused to do as he was told.

Like most children who seek to test their parents' will, this started as the smallest of rebellions—refusal to eat the last spoonful of his meal, unwillingness to share his toys with his siblings, tantrums at bedtime when he wasn't allowed to stay up as late or play outside as long as the older children.

Jherl's parents had seen such behavior before, in their other children, and knew it was only a matter of time and patience before the boy grew out of his childish ways. This, they knew, was the way of children, and it did not worry them unduly to see the spark of resistance in their youngest boy. Thus, they chided him as parents should, and ignored the worst of his sour attitude, and longed for the time when the child would learn the error of his ways and come to understand the virtues of being well behaved and obeying the will of those older and wiser than himself.

Yet the weeks and months passed by, and still the child continued with his willful behavior. Soon the parents grew tired and dismayed, for try as they might, they could not find the means to control him. The boy grew sullen and quiet, for he was shunned by his peers and siblings alike, as none could stand to be associated with the boy for fear that they, too, might be seen as unruly.

No matter what they said, his parents could not convince Jherl to see sense. The boy seemed deaf to all reason, and while his mother recognized that it was good for a young man to show spirit, Jherl's behavior, she feared, was becoming problematic, and if he was not careful, it might attract the wrong kind of attention to their family—for she had heard tell of the Dark Wraith and his vengeance, and she knew that Jherl's misbehavior risked bringing his wrath down upon them.

Jherl's mother spoke to the boy of her fears, warning him to be wary, as, for all they knew, the Dark Wraith might already be watching, stirring in the darkness, ready to strike the boy down. At that the boy laughed, for he was not of a superstitious nature and believed his mother was merely attempting to scare him into abandoning his rebellious ways and doing as she and his father commanded. To him, the Dark Wraith was nothing more than a story to be easily ignored, an old legend designed to frighten the naïve.

So it was that the boy continued down his wayward path, objecting to the word of any and all authority figures, refusing to complete his lessons or obey rules, and failing to complete chores, while disregarding all that his parents said.

Others wondered how the boy had gotten away with such blatant misbehavior for so long, why the Dark Wraith had not come for him in the night, but it soon became clear that the Dark Wraith had merely been biding his time.

There came an evening when Jherl, grown exceedingly bold and outlandish in his misbehavior, decided he would break into the stores of a nearby merchant and help himself to the man's wares. Jherl, being only ten, was still small and lithe, and thus was able to wriggle his way into the merchant's stores by way of a broken window. Once inside, he sought out the sweetest delicacies he could find and, with no concern for the consequences, began to feast, gasping in pleasure as he stuffed handful after handful into his mouth. To Jherl, the food tasted all the sweeter for having been stolen in that way, and he laughed at his own cleverness, already plotting his next nefarious scheme.

Only, the Dark Wraith had indeed been watching Jherl's descent into criminality, and, breath rasping like some dreadful, monstrous beast, he threw open the doors to the stores with a flick of his wrist and burst in, his red arm flashing in the darkness, words of vengeance echoing from his horrible grated mouth.

The following morning the merchant, upon visiting his stores to replenish his stock, found to his horror that Jherl's mother's worst fears had come true: the boy had been visited by the Dark Wraith in the night and duly punished.

Another story tells of a young girl, Marionette, who had been doted upon all her life by her mother and father, the singular object of their affection, but in having gained recognition for her academic talents had been taken into a residential academy for the talented and gifted.

Marionette was not a bad student—indeed, in many ways she was held in the highest esteem by her teachers for her precision and punctuality—and yet, having once been the center of attention, she found it difficult to adjust to her new position amongst the other students, expected to share and demonstrate friendship, kindness, and understanding. Marionette saw these traits only as weaknesses and refused to comply with the fundamental tenets of the academy. She believed herself to be above the rules, immune to punishment—*set apart*—and so began her slow journey to insurrection as she disregarded all that was asked of her by her teachers and fellow pupils.

The other children could not understand this capricious behavior, but Marionette would not hear a word of reason and, indeed, began a campaign of terror against those who would speak out. This manifested in such ill behavior as pushing and shoving, name-calling, and stealing other students' work.

Soon Marionette's parents were summoned to the academy to talk reason to the girl. Appalled, they warned her of the terror she was courting, for the Dark Wraith was surely watching and might come at any moment to punish her for what she had done.

Marionette, of course, maintained that the Dark Wraith would never come for her, for she was set apart and even *his* rules could never apply to her.

Such arrogance proved to be her downfall. One night soon after, the other girls in the dormitory awoke to the horrifying sound of the Dark Wraith's rasping breath as he came for Marionette in the darkness.

All who witnessed it described him as a figure of purest shadow, emerging from the darkness like a nightmare given flesh. His face was a terrible, eyeless visage, and his arm burned red like the fires of hate, humming with terrible, exotic power. The sound that accompanied his passing was like no other sound in the galaxy—half machine, half man, like the rush of air before an explosion, like the universe itself drawing breath.

The girls knew, then, that Marionette would never be seen again, and as they ran for cover, screaming for their elders, the Dark Wraith stole the misbehaving girl away, whisking her off into the night.

Of course, tales of the Dark Wraith's punishment

were not reserved for children alone, and as word of his exploits spread, there were many adults who succumbed to his judgment, too, such as the notorious gambler Kup'bree'ak.

Kup'bree'ak was a Togruta who had come to Solace to seek his fortune at the gaming tables that once filled the glittering casinos of the city's lofty spires. He was a devious fellow, and although he'd arrived with barely enough credits to pay for a single week's board, within three months he was one of the wealthiest gamblers in the city. Anyone who asked was told that this was purely down to his instinct at the tables, and perhaps a little luck, but many suspected there was more to Kup'bree'ak's rise to fortune than was widely known.

Indeed, it eventually transpired that the Togruta was not beyond hiring thugs and gangsters to press his potential opponents to throw their games, using blackmail or threats of violence. He was thought, too, to have struck a deal with the owners of at least three of the casinos—a deal that saw Kup'bree'ak deliver quite a winning streak but also saw those same casinos make significant gains.

Word soon got around that Kup'bree'ak had a habit of playing dirty, and yet few could understand how he continued to find wealthy opponents willing to take him on. This, of course, was down to the work of his gangster friends, who continued to find means to twist his opponents' arms—often literally.

Kup'bree'ak was not the first to cheat at the gambling tables, and most certainly not the last, but his strong-arm tactics proved his downfall when, during a confrontation behind a casino one night, gangsters in the Togruta's employ, intending to rough up another opponent, accidentally killed the man.

Hearing of this, Kup'bree'ak merely shrugged, for he had not, after all, been present when the heinous act was committed, and there were no means by which the authorities of Solace could associate him with the crime.

The Dark Wraith, however, was not bound by such empirical evidence, for he alone had insight into the souls and minds of his victims and might see the truth of what had occurred.

As such, the Dark Wraith, a vision of dread that emerged from Kup'bree'ak's coin vault as he sought to count his winnings, poured his wrath upon the Togruta that very night. Kup'bree'ak pleaded for mercy, but the Dark Wraith had no concept of the word, and his red forelimb brought only death for the gambler who had misbehaved so grievously.

Yet despite word of the Dark Wraith's vengeance spreading, most in Solace ignored these dire warnings and, far from dissuaded, continued to go about their business, allowing misbehavior to flourish in their midst.

No one knows what terrible deed triggered the Dark Wraith's final act of punishment upon Solace, or whether it was simply an accumulation of continued bad behavior amongst the citizens, but one stormy night, it is said that the Dark Wraith rose up in anger and in his rage set upon the city itself, tearing down all that he could see.

Those who saw him ran in fear, but to no avail. His

power was boundless, and he cast them aside with a flick of his wrist and toppled buildings in his wake. The screams of his victims could be heard throughout the city as he cut a swathe through the populace, striking down all in his path. For the Dark Wraith knew only vengeance, and he sought to send a warning to those in the neighboring cities who might still consider rebelling.

The people hoped beyond hope that the Wanderer might return to save them—for Solace had three times in the past been visited by a kindly figure who had helped protect the people from harm—but it was clear he had vanished, or else was powerless to face the Dark Wraith, for he did not come, and the wave of utter destruction continued unopposed. Fires burned, and the ground itself seemed to open, swallowing tenements and towers, palaces and parks, as all around them withered and died.

Within the space of a single night, the entire city had been destroyed, its people wiped out. All that was left was in ruin. The Dark Wraith had disappeared, fading into the shadows to return to his terrible realm of fire and magma, and the city was silent, save for the sound of a few mewling animals still walking the devastated streets.

Scant few had survived the onslaught of the Dark Wraith, and those few knew they had been spared only so word might spread to the other cities and all might learn to stay in line, certain in the knowledge of what awaited them if they did not.

So the lesson was learned, and those in the city of Mock have, for generations, lived in fear of the Dark Wraith's return. Parents there do all in their power to ensure that their children are well behaved and understand the consequences of defiance. It is whispered amongst them that if any are brave enough to visit the ruins of Solace, the echo of the Dark Wraith's rasping breath might still be heard, low and menacing.

Such is the risk of rebellion, for the Dark Wraith lies in wait to be summoned, ready to punish all who are deserving.

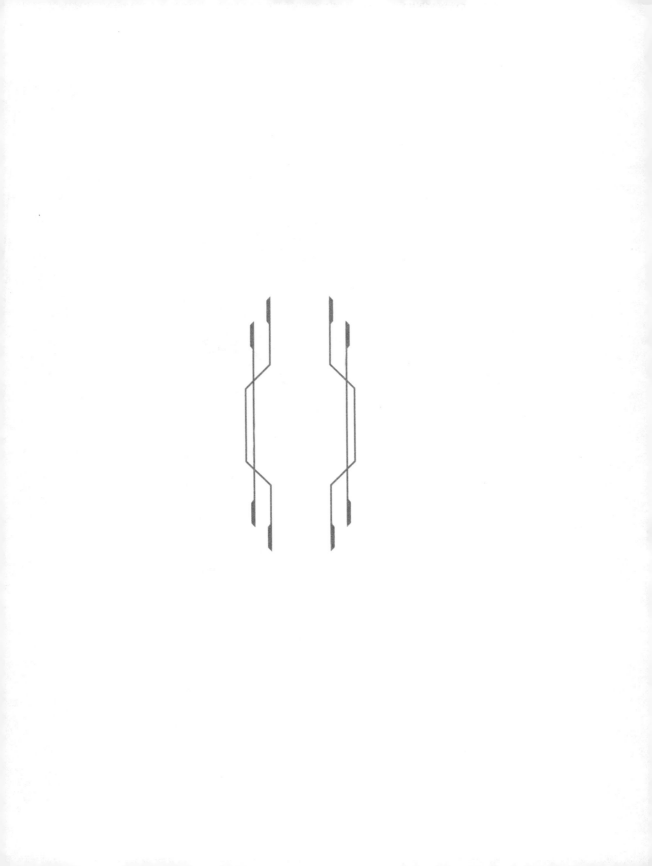

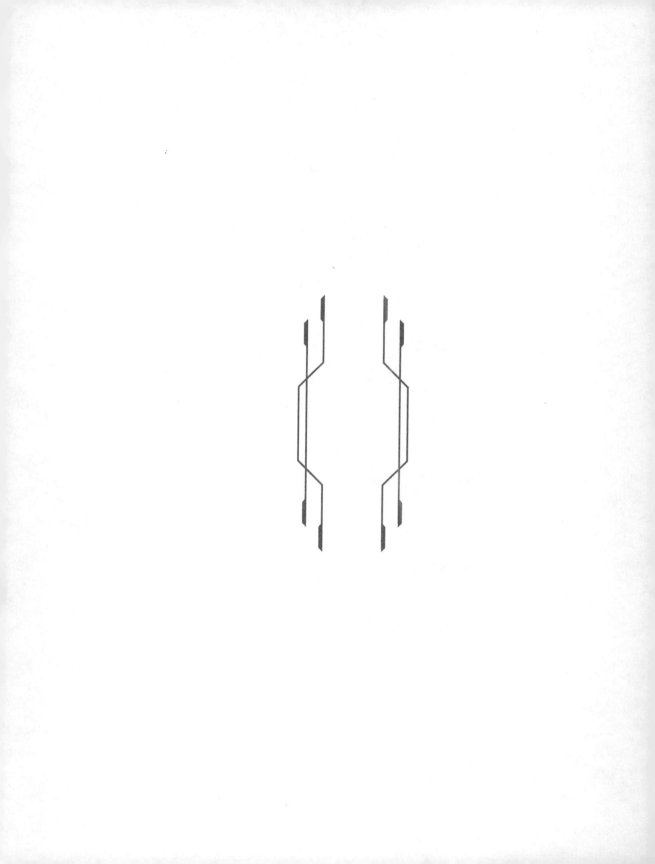

CHASING

GHOSTS

HERE WAS ONCE A SCOUN-
drel named Misook, who, pursued by
a bounty hunter for reneging on a deal
with a notorious crime boss on the
ice world Kaspas, fled to the planet Batuu in the Outer
Rim, hopeful that he might shake his pursuer amongst
the black spires and murky alleyways of the infamous
outpost.

Misook was a cunning but arrogant man and knew
that, if only he could cover his trail, he might make use
of Batuu as a staging post, a port from where he could
disappear into the depths of Wild Space to pursue his
fortune, far from the enemies he had made for himself
at home.

Yet the bounty hunter—a Mirialan named Emim'Ai—
was dogged and persistent in her pursuit of Misook,

for she was young and still making a name for herself amongst the criminal houses who served as her patrons. In pursuing Misook, she saw that she might prove herself worthy of an even bigger bounty and acquire a valuable reputation.

Misook, impressed with the bounty hunter's tenacity, took great care to seed misdirection in his wake, altering passenger manifests, greasing the palms of unscrupulous smugglers, and adopting a growing number of outland-ish personas and disguises. None of that proved enough, however, as Emim'Ai seemed to have a preternatural ability to seek him out, anticipating his every move, unmasking his every disguise, and following him from port to port, right across the galaxy.

Once, the woman even came close to catching her quarry as the two of them battled in the dark backstreets of Lothal, dancing and weaving down the narrow lanes and around the steaming outlet pipes, each of their moves a perfect match for the other's. Then, just when it had seemed the bounty hunter would get the better

of him, Misook had fled in a stolen speeder, zipping off through the bustling markets and out into the wastelands beyond. Emim'Ai, of course, went after him, only ever a few steps behind.

So it had continued for many months, and although Misook had hoped the Mirialan might eventually grow weary of the chase and break off her pursuit, it was not to be. The bounty hunter, he knew, could not return empty-handed to those who had charged her with his capture.

Batuu, then, was to be the site of their final dance, for Misook knew that he could not run forever and that, if he were ever to succeed in making a new life for himself, he would have to find a means to deal with his determined pursuer, once and for all.

As relentless as Emim'Ai had been, and as hungry to prove herself, it occurred to Misook that the only way to shake her was to distract her with an even bigger prize—a bounty so large and so notorious that she would not be able to resist its allure. It just so happened

that, on Batuu, the perfect opportunity presented itself.

Misook, for all his dubious ways, was a born orator, so on his third night at the Black Spire Outpost, having recognized the bounty hunter's ship in the dock and obtained word that she was asking after him in many of the less-than-salubrious places around town, he decided to enact his final move.

He found a table in a quiet corner of Oga's Cantina—a corner with a full view of the bar—and, after making merry with a number of the other patrons, buying drinks and regaling them with tales of his exploits, he began to weave the tale of Arquel.

Arquel, in his mind, was the most remarkable thief ever to have traversed the galaxy—a woman who had incurred the wrath of scores of lords, ladies, and crime bosses throughout known space and beyond. Hers was a name that was whispered by bounty hunters far and wide, from Coruscant to Naboo, from Mandalore to Glee Anselm. This thief had a combined price on her head so large that anyone who captured her alive would have enough credits to buy their own moon. But Arquel was clever and quick and wise, and could never be caught. Tales of her derring-do were the talk of cantina patrons and smugglers, traders, pilots, and politicians. Yet she was like a ghost: gone before her targets knew they had been robbed, always disappearing into the night before anyone had even caught a glimpse of her.

Soon, intrigued by his talk of this great thief, a large audience had gathered around Misook's table, urging him to relate her tale. So, making himself comfortable, he leaned back in his seat, put his feet up on the table and his hands behind his head, and started from the very beginning. . . .

Arquel was born in the sump canyons of distant Coruscant, down amongst the lowest levels, where the streets are cast in a perpetual night and the veneer of civilization barely hides the festering nightmare of daily life.

This was in the days following the fall of the great Empire, and although many throughout the galaxy felt the yoke of oppression

had finally lifted, for those eking out an existence in the forgotten levels amidst the sewers and outlet pipes, life continued as it always had: a constant battle to obtain another meal.

Arquel's mother was a thief who barely managed to stay a step ahead of the private security forces who patrolled those levels (the official law enforcement agencies refused to delve so deep into the fetid criminal morass), and her father was a disgraced administrator from the Imperial era who worked as a translator for the criminal gangs, hiring out his services for a price cheaper than that of a battered old protocol droid.

Arquel, then, had not been granted the best start in life and as a child was often to be found assisting her mother on smaller jobs, wriggling through tiny crawlspaces and ventilation shafts to open doors, lay traps, or provide distraction. As such, she learned her craft at an early age, and it was this apprenticeship that provided her with the skills she would later employ to such great effect. If her mother gave her anything in life, it was this grounding in the finer arts of thievery and deception.

As she grew, however, Arquel became less useful to her mother, and while her father was off on business, she was often

left to her own devices. Resourceful, though, she put the time to opportune use, familiarizing herself with the secret passageways and alcoves of the neighborhood, observing all the comings and goings, listening to all the many whispered conversations. Later, she would learn how to put the information she gleaned from those overheard meetings to good use—discerning patterns of behavior, collating secrets, fathoming plans. She would sell this information to interested parties or blackmail those who wished to keep their secretive dealings undisclosed. She never told her parents about her ill-gotten gains, and in time she had gathered not only a small fund of her own but also something of a reputation amongst the criminal gangs who made the sump canyons their home.

By the age of fifteen, Arquel was running with the Hutt Clan, and while she'd begun her new career doing much the same as she always had—farming information and passing it up the chain to those in charge—she'd also made quite an impression, proving herself to be a most valuable and trusted asset. So much so that the rival gangs had taken note and begun to formulate plans of their own.

It was around this time that the young woman learned the value—and cost—of betrayal.

Out on a job one night with a Weequay named Malquis, Arquel found herself party to a deal between two gangs. One crime lord wished to purchase from another the hilt of a broken lightsaber, scavenged from the ruins of Geonosis and traded back and forth between the criminal gangs of Coruscant as a symbol of their power and influence. Arquel and Malquis were to make the exchange, handing over a datachip containing dubious access codes to an upper-level administration building and returning with the saber's hilt as their prize. At the moment of the exchange, none other than Arquel's mother revealed herself from the shadows, having followed her daughter, and she intercepted the exchange, shooting Malquis and the members of the other gang and making off with both the datachip and the lightsaber.

Arquel, abandoned in the devastation, was left to explain herself to her employer and endure the painful punishment for her failure. Yet the betrayal hardened Arquel, like a sword tempered in flame, and she sought out her mother later that week, ambushing the woman in return and striking her down, relieving

her of both the datachip and the lightsaber hilt—and her relationship with her daughter.

Having keenly felt the punishment bestowed upon her by her employer, however, Arquel chose not to return to him with her trophies, but instead used the datachip to strike a deal of her own, purchasing transport offworld so she might at last take to the stars and make a life and name for herself in the wider galaxy.

Of the lightsaber hilt, it is said that she still wears it to this day, attached to her belt, a constant reminder of her mother's betrayal and what might happen if she ever trusts anyone again.

From there, it becomes harder to piece together Arquel's exact movements, but sometime after leaving Coruscant, she acquired her own ship, an old customized transport piloted by a reprogrammed RX pilot droid that she stole from a bounty hunter named Popundas Heth.

Years passed, and Arquel became famed on a score of worlds, wanted by criminals and authorities alike. Nevertheless, she operated with apparent impunity, carrying out daring raids and making singular deals with even the most notorious gangsters. She traversed the galaxy, taking all she wanted, always staying

one step ahead of those who pursued her, always with a smile and a wink and a flash of a deadly weapon.

Many have taken up the trail of Arquel, hoping to achieve glory in her safe capture, but to this date, all have failed. No one knows where she will turn up next, for she has never been seen in the same place twice, but (and this was the moment Misook had been building up to all that time) *she was last seen on Batuu, in the very cantina in which we sit, just two days ago. . . .*

Misook was wily, and he knew that, for his story to take root, he needed to play his own part in the tale; so while his audience babbled excitedly about the celebrity who had walked in their midst, he outlined his own plan to capture her—for, he claimed, he was a bounty hunter from Coruscant, a member of one of those original gangs, and as much as he pursued Arquel for wealth, he pursued her, too, for revenge. There, on Batuu, he would finally deliver it.

As the crowd broke apart, Misook made his escape

from the cantina, yet he knew from the overheard mumblings of the other patrons that word of Arquel would spread. Sure enough, the next morning, talk of the thief was on everyone's lips, and even the news feeds were running stories about the sighting of the dangerous woman, warning any who saw her to approach the authorities rather than try their hand at restraining her themselves. Of course, there were those amongst the people of the Outpost who were formulating their own plans, for word of the size of the bounty on Arquel's head had spread, too. Bounty hunters, vagabonds, gangsters, and scoundrels alike were plotting her capture—including Emim'Ai, who had traveled to Batuu in pursuit of Misook but had set her sights on the bigger bounty that was just within her reach.

Laughing, Misook made for the docks, plotting a course into Wild Space, where he knew he might start his life anew.

Throughout Batuu, the hunt for Arquel continued for several weeks, until an administrator at the docks turned up a record of an old customized transport that had visited the Outpost around the same time as Misook but had left in a hurry, logging a course into Wild Space.

Of course, many of the bounty hunters, including Emim'Ai, gave chase, but none found Arquel, or Misook, and soon rumor had spread throughout the entire galaxy of this elusive legend—the biggest score in the galaxy, the most sought-after bounty of all.

To this day, people seek the mysterious Arquel, telling tales of her exploits, of how one day she disappeared in Wild Space, pursued by a bounty hunter who was never heard from again.

Only Misook, sitting somewhere with his feet up in a cantina, laughing, knows the truth: that she never really existed at all.

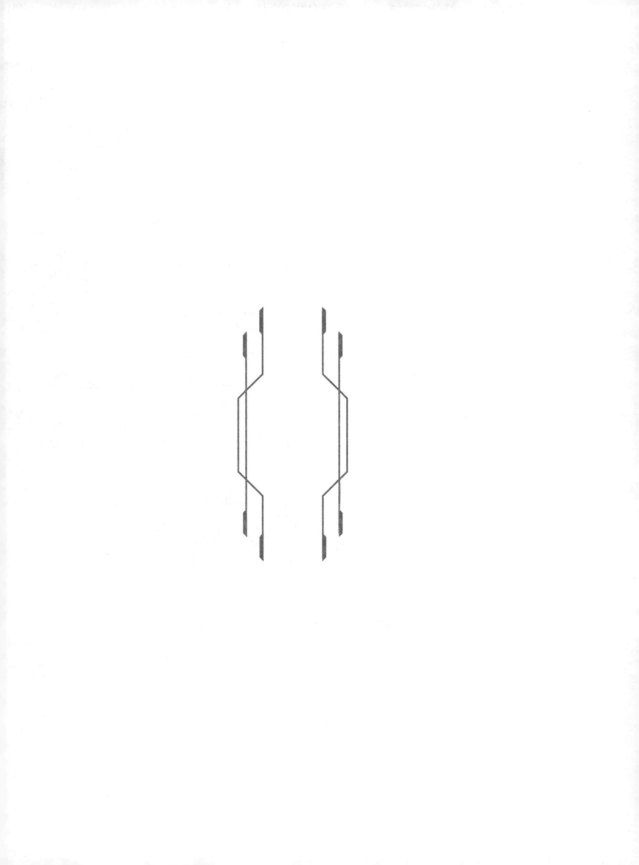

ABOUT THE AUTHOR

GEORGE MANN is a *Sunday Times* best-selling novelist and scriptwriter, and he's loved *Star Wars* for about as long as he's been able to walk. He wishes he still had the Ewok village action figure set he adored when he was a boy.

He's the author of the Newbury & Hobbes Victorian mystery series, as well as four novels about a 1920s vigilante known as the Ghost. He's also written best-selling *Doctor Who* novels, new adventures for Sherlock Holmes, and the supernatural mystery series Wychwood.

His comic writing includes extensive work on *Doctor Who, Dark Souls, Warhammer 40,000,* and *Newbury &*

Hobbes, as well as *Teenage Mutant Ninja Turtles* for younger readers.

He's written audio scripts for *Doctor Who, Blake's 7, Sherlock Holmes, Warhammer 40,000,* and more.

As editor, he's assembled four anthologies of original Sherlock Holmes fiction, as well as multiple volumes of *The Solaris Book of New Science Fiction* and *The Solaris Book of New Fantasy.*

You can find him on Twitter @George_Mann.

ABOUT THE ARTIST

GRANT GRIFFIN is an illustrator working in games and publishing. He grew up outside of Austin, Texas, and did a stint in Denver, Colorado, where he got a BFA in illustration, found a wife, got a dog, and took up a career freelancing in 2013. He has since been carving out a niche in the fantasy and science fiction genre. He resides in San Juan del Sur, Nicaragua, and does his best not to indulge in too much local coffee.

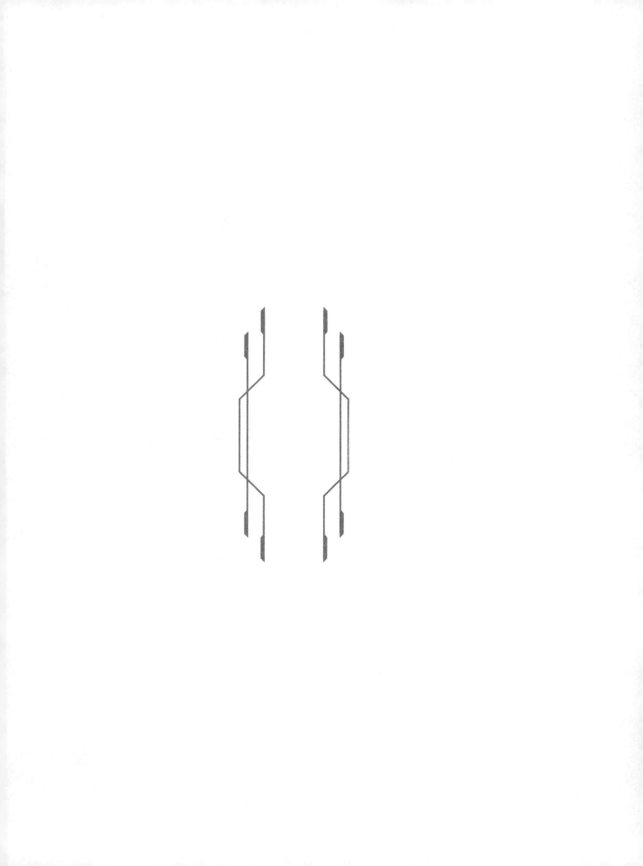

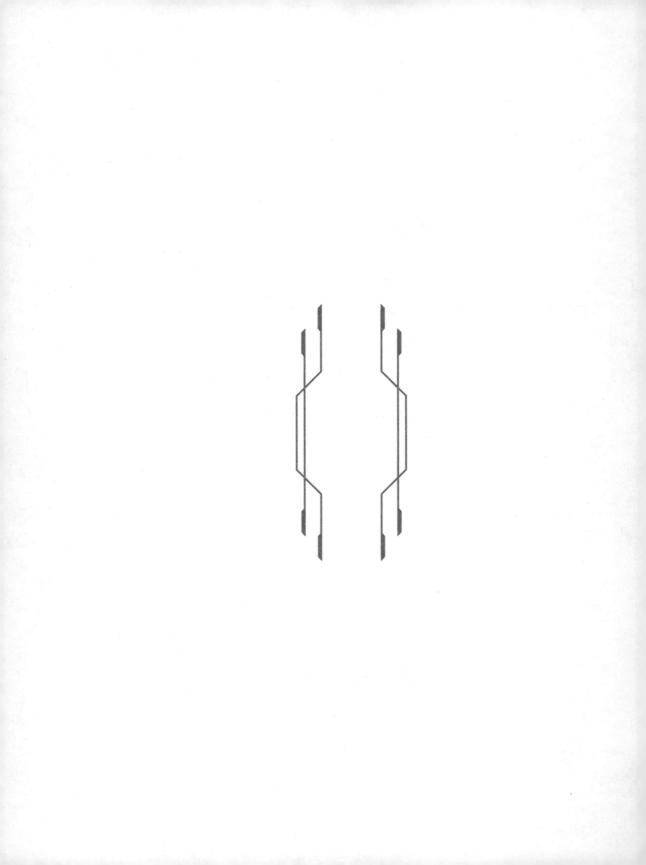